BONAVENTURE

THE CROSSROAD SPIRITUAL LEGACY SERIES
Edited by John Farina

The Rule of Benedict: Insights for the Ages
    by Joan Chittister, O.S.B.

Ignatius Loyola: Spiritual Exercises
    by Joseph A. Tetlow, S.J.

Francis de Sales: Introduction to the Devout Life
and Treatise on the Love of God
    by Wendy M. Wright

Teresa of Avila: Mystical Writings
    by Tessa Bielecki

St. Francis of Assisi: Writings for a Gospel Life
    by Regis J. Armstrong, O.F.M. Cap.

Augustine: Essential Writings
    by Benedict J. Groeschel, C.S.R.

Thomas Aquinas: Spiritual Master
    by Robert Barron

Hildegard: Prophet of the Cosmic Christ
    by Renate Craine

Karl Rahner: Mystic of Everyday Life
    by Harvey D. Egan

C.S. Lewis: Spirituality for Mere Christians
    by William Griffin

Anselm: The Joy of Faith
    by William Shannon

Dante Alighieri: Divine Comedy, *Divine Spirituality*
    by Robert Royal

John of the Cross: Doctor of Light and Love
    by Kieran Kavanaugh, O.C.D.

BONAVENTURE

MYSTICAL WRITINGS

Zachary Hayes

A Crossroad Book
The Crossroad Publishing Company
New York

The Crossroad Publishing Company
370 Lexington Avenue, New York, NY 10017

Printed in the United States of America

Library of Congress Cataloging-in-Publication Data

Hayes, Zachary.
    Bonaventure : mystical writings / Zachary Hayes.
        p.   cm. — (The Crossroad spiritual legacy series)
    Includes bibliographical references (p.   ).
    ISBN 0-8245-2514-0
    1. Bonaventure, Saint, Cardinal, ca. 1217–1274.   2. Theology,
Doctrinal—History—Middle Ages, 600–1500.   I. Title.   II. Series.
BX4700.B68H39   1999
230'.2'092—dc21   99-14481
                                                          CIP

1   2   3   4   5   6   7   8   9   10   03   02   01   00   99

Dedicated to
my dear friend
Dr. M. Therese Southgate,
whose search for a unified vision
in her personal journey
echoes so many of the themes in
Bonaventure's work

Contents

Foreword

Bonaventure. If asked to identify him, I would wager that most educated persons would at least recognize the name. Yet he is certainly not as familiar as many of the other figures that have been featured in the Spiritual Legacy series to date. The memory of people like Augustine, Benedict, Francis of Assisi, Aquinas, and Ignatius Loyola have, for various reasons, endured in our culture even to the point of having scores of cities, schools, and hospitals dedicated to their memories. Their books are read, their poetry recited, their prayers still offered. Yet in terms of the quality of his intellectual achievements, Bonaventure was their equal. His work won for him the title of a great master of the spiritual life: a Doctor of the Church. Discovering him, then, is somewhat like making the acquaintance of a distant member of the family who, we discover after finally meeting him, has had a brilliant and celebrated career.

Bonaventure lived in the thirteenth century, a time when the learning of the monastic orders had found new homes outside of the monasteries, in the universities established in the great cities of Europe. At Paris he taught on the faculty where another Italian scholar, Thomas Aquinas, would make his monumental contribution to Western civilization. But Bonaventure was not a member of one of the orders with a long tradition of scholarship such as the Dominicans or the Benedictines. Rather, he was a follower of Francis of Assisi. *Il Poverello* was anything but a professional academic. An itinerant preacher who lived by the radical teachings of the Gospels, a prophet, a wandering holy man—Francis was all of these things, and so were the majority of his followers. It was not his writings—which were minimal—but his actions that became the basis of a powerful renewal movement.

Francis had modeled a new awareness of the presence of God in creation. It made him write odes to Brother Sun, and in our own day has won for him the title of patron saint of environmentalism. Bonaventure, as a follower of Francis, had lived that new insight. His task as a Franciscan and an academic was to explore the implications of Francis's spirituality for philosophy and theology. He did that with a passion and strength that immediately confront even the most casual reader of his texts. When he was finished, he had produced a highly detailed map that charted new ground for both the intellect seeking understanding and the heart seeking love.

The author of this volume, Zachary Hayes, like Bonaventure, is both a follower of St. Francis and a professional scholar. His presentation of Bonaventure has the balance and nuance that only years of studying and living the tradition could bring. In it the richness of an age in which the inner workings of the human intellect—its powers of reasoning and of understanding, of desiring and of loving—were all seen as reflections of the macrocosm, not the idiosyncrasies of the individual, a time when creation and the divine were linked, and when human love was seen as a reflection of the love that made the stars.

It is then with special delight that I present this volume and ask, in the words of Bonaventure that you

> Open your eyes,
> Alert your spiritual ears,
> Unseal your lips,
> And apply your heart!

John Farina

Preface

In line with the general policy of this series, this volume is an attempt to provide an orientation and an introduction to some of the outstanding texts of a great spiritual writer and theologian from the Christian tradition. In this case, we are dealing with a Franciscan, St. Bonaventure. Bonaventure has left a wealth of written materials and takes a consistently philosophical approach to matters of theology and spirituality; this can make our task difficult.

The task of situating Bonaventure's thought in its historical context might well be compared to what many today call a cross-cultural experience. The seven hundred years that separate us just happen to place Bonaventure in a pre-Enlightenment context and ourselves in a very different post-Enlightenment context. Hence, we can easily see the difficulty of trying to enter his world from our perspective.

In planning this book, two distinct approaches seemed possible. One possibility was to provide a literary introduction to each of the many texts of Bonaventure that deal with spirituality and mysticism. Since there are a significant number of such texts, this would have been a rather forbidding task and may not have provided a good sense of what Bonaventure's system looks like as a whole. The other option was to use the basic structure of a single text that comes closest to providing a synthesis of his thought in his own terms, and to discuss the topics related to that structure by drawing other texts into the picture. This is the way we have chosen. The structure is taken from *The Journey of the Soul into God.*

The other texts are taken from a wide range of Bonaventure's systematic and spiritual writings.

At times these selections are quite brief; at other times they are rather lengthy. The author's intention is to place them in an expository context that will help open them to the reader. Precisely because of the distance between Bonaventure's time and our own, the expository material frequently goes into considerable detail. Though the style—both Bonaventure's and mine—will be difficult at times, my hope is that it will be very rewarding when the richness and depth of his thought begin to open before us. My hope is not so much to simplify the work of a challenging thinker and mystical author as to make some of his insightful and powerful texts available to a wider reading public.

During the time I have been working on this book, the thought constantly came to my mind that this book would never have been written without the pioneering work of Fr. Philotheus Boehner, O.F.M. Though I never had the pleasure of meeting him personally, much of my introduction to medieval Franciscan theology and spirituality was based on his work. His translation of the *Journey of the Soul into God,* together with a very rich commentary, is still my vademecum for that particular work.

After my seminary studies, I was introduced into quite different dimensions of Bonaventure's work through the study of Joseph Cardinal Ratzinger, who had recently completed a major study on Bonaventure's theology of history when I arrived in Germany to pursue doctoral studies in theology. Cardinal Ratzinger was one of my professors at the University of Bonn. From him I have learned much about the problems raised by the diverse readings of the work of Joachim of Fiore and the relation of this to the later work of Bonaventure, culminating in the *Collations on the Six Days of Creation.*

During the years of my own personal investigation of the Seraphic Doctor, the friendship and scholarship of both Ewert Cousins and Bernard McGinn have been a constant stimulus and support. Without all of these exceptional people, this book would never have been written.

Finally, I would like to say a word of thanks to Crossroad Publishing Company for undertaking this exceptional series, and for inviting me to make a contribution to it. It is my sincere hope that, in line with the rationale of the series, my work will help make the spiritual doctrine of one of the great masters accessible to many people today at a time when so many are searching for a deeper understanding of their life and of their relation with the divine.

Zachary Hayes, O.F.M.
Catholic Theological Union
Chicago, Illinois

Abbreviations

Brevil.	*Breviloquium*
DM	*Defense of the Mendicants*
GS	*Collations on the Gifts of the Holy Spirit*
JS	*The Journey of the Soul into God*
KC	*Disputed Questions on the Knowledge of Christ*
LM	*The Major Life of St. Francis*
LMin	*The Minor Life of St. Francis*
MV	*Mystical Vine*
PL	*On the Perfection of Life*
RA	*On the Reduction of the Arts to Theology*
SD	*Collations on the Six Days of Creation*
Sent.	*Commentary on the Sentences*
Solil.	*Soliloquium*
TL	*Tree of Life*
Trin.	*Disputed Questions on the Mystery of the Trinity*
TW	*The Threefold Way*

Introduction

When I first visited the remnants of the medieval town of Bagnoregio, I was stunned by the impact of the terrain. It might best be described as a very large crater with a cone standing in the center. On top of that cone are the ruins of the ancient town known as Bagnoregio, the birthplace of St. Bonaventure. When one stands in that town today, no matter which direction one looks, one is looking out from the center to the circumference of the circular crater. It is not clear how much of the present geographical character is due to an earthquake that hit the region in the year 1695. But as the town now stands, it is a powerful symbol of one of the driving metaphors of St. Bonaventure's theology and spirituality: that is, the symbol of the circle with its circumference and center. God can be thought of as "an intelligible sphere whose center is everywhere, and whose circumference is nowhere" (*JS* 5.8 [5:310]).

Working with this symbol, Bonaventure can speak of a center in God. And it is through that center that God reaches out to form the created world. The world with its history, then, moves outward in a circular movement from its origin in God to find its final end in its return to God. This circular movement is mediated by the central person of the Trinity, who became incarnate in the form of Jesus of Nazareth, thereby bringing the center of God into union with the center of the world.

Precisely how Bonaventure himself came to this vision we may never know. But to anyone who visits the place of his birth today, the physical ruins stand as a remarkable symbol of the vision that eventually emanated from the spirit and mind of this exceptional human being.

The Life and Works of St. Bonaventure

Not a lot is known about the saint's youth. Scholars are not sure of the exact year of his birth, but it is placed between 1217 and 1221. At baptism he was given the name Giovanni after his father, Giovanni di Fidanza, who worked as a doctor in Bagnoregio. His mother was Maria Ritella.

His earliest education was probably with the friars at Bagnoregio. After some ten years with them, he moved to Paris in 1235 or 1236 to begin the study of the arts. It was in Paris, probably in the year 1243, that he entered the Franciscan Order and began the study of theology during the time of Alexander of Hales, John of La Rochelle, Odo Rigaldi, and William of Meliton. He became a Bachelor of Scripture in 1248 and commented on the *Sentences* of Peter Lombard from 1250 to 1252. From 1253 to 1257, he functioned as regent master for the school of the Franciscans at Paris and became one of the most impressive representatives of the early Franciscan theology at the University of Paris, though he describes himself merely as a "poor and weak compiler" (*II Sent.* prael. [2:1]).

His early writings, which come from this period, consist largely of scriptural commentaries and his monumental *Commentary on the Sentences.* Together with these, there are three sets of disputed questions: *On the Knowledge of Christ, On the Mystery of the Trinity,* and *On Evangelical Perfection.* These works, while they are cast in a strictly academic style, provide important insights into many of the concerns that will appear in his later works that deal specifically with spirituality.

During those years, the Franciscan Order was torn by volatile disputes concerning the nature of the order and its relation to St. Francis of Assisi. In this context, thirty-one years after the death of St. Francis, Bonaventure was elected minister general of the order on February 2, 1257. This took him out of the academic context and placed him directly in the work of administration for the rest of his life. It was probably during this time, or very close to the end of his university career, that he wrote the *Breviloquium,* which is seen by many medieval scholars to be a particularly impressive *summa* of medieval, systematic theology in a single volume.

While he continued to make his headquarters at Paris, Bonaventure traveled widely to visit the friars in Germany, England, Spain, and Italy, attempting to mediate among the friars concerning the burning differences that divided them. Early in his years as general, in 1259, he visited Mount Alverna, the place of St. Francis's stigmatization. This was a most intense experience for Bonaventure in his efforts to come to a better understanding of St. Francis, and out of it was to come the spiritual classic known as *The Journey of the Soul into God.*

This work will play a major role in our presentation of Bonaventure's orientation to spirituality. While the basic structure of this work reveals the significant influence of Richard of St. Victor, it is, in another sense, a very personal synthesis of Bonaventure's own journey, viewed now in relation to the experience of St. Francis. In a rich symbolic structure, the book brings together central elements of the spirituality of the saint of Assisi with other styles of Christian spirituality and the personal experience of Bonaventure, the scholar and friar, and now the minister general of the order. Of particular significance in the shaping of this text, apart from Richard of St. Victor, is the work of St. Augustine and that of Pseudo-Dionysius.

Later writings of Bonaventure are the *Defense of the Mendicants,* the *Soliloquium,* the *Threefold Way,* the *Tree of Life,* the *Mystical Vine, Five Feasts of the Child Jesus, On the Perfection of Life,* the *Life of St. Francis,* numerous sermons, especially those on St. Francis, the *Collations on the Ten Commandments,* the *Collations on the Gifts of the Holy Spirit,* and the *Collations on the Six Days of Creation,* his final work, which was left unfinished because of Bonaventure's elevation to the cardinalate. Most of these works will play a significant role in our presentation.

For our purpose here, the technical term *collation* can be taken as equivalent to a theological conference commonly cast in the form of a sermon and given after luncheon or in the evening to an audience of masters, bachelors, and friars of various sorts connected with the university.

In 1273, Bonaventure was named cardinal bishop of Albano by Pope Gregory X. From this point on he was concerned with the preparations for the Council of Lyons, which convened in May of 1274. He was an active participant in the work of the council until his unexpected death on July 15, 1274. In 1482 he was canonized, and in 1588 he was given the title Seraphic Doctor, a designation that highlights one of the basic qualities of his teaching. The seraph is understood to be the highest of the traditional choirs of angels, whose nature is the purest love. Hence, in Christian iconography, the seraph is commonly used as a symbol of love.

The Context of Bonaventure's Work

It is clear that no system of theology or spirituality exists in a vacuum. Bonaventure was a person who was deeply involved in many of the crucial issues in the life of medieval Europe, and specifically in the life of the Franciscan Order. The period in which St. Francis lived and in which the Franciscan Order began was marked by a variety of reform movements involving sectarian groups with a strongly heretical nature. The "Poor Men of Lyons" may be seen as an instance of a reform movement bearing a striking resemblance to the Franciscans which eventually found itself outside the official church. Such movements raised serious questions about how one was to understand any spirituality that thought of itself as a form of the imitation of Christ. This would be one of the major questions raised by the secular masters in university circles during the career of Bonaventure, and he dealt with it at length in his *Disputed Questions on Evangelical Perfection* as well as later in his *Defense of the Mendicants.*

The movement known as Catharism involved an emphatic form of dualism, seeing material reality as essentially evil and as the work of an evil principle. This raises questions not only about the human body but also about the material beings in the world of creation as a whole. It is often argued, and for good reasons, that the *Canticle of Creatures* of St. Francis of Assisi is the saint's way of responding to Catharism. This might be seen as the context for a spirituality such as Bonaventure's, which, as we shall see, takes the whole of the created world, both material and spiritual, as a theophany.

Joachim of Fiore, the famous Calabrian abbot, in the light of a special experience which he claimed to have had on Pentecost Sunday, presented a new theology of history that would eventually be taken up by some radical Franciscans as a framework for developing their own program for the order and the church. These would be known as the Franciscan Joachites. Their understanding would lead to divisive issues for the order. At one level these were problems internal to the order, for they concerned the order's own proper self-understanding. But when that self-understanding was cast in the potentially incendiary terms of the radical Joachite Franciscans, they became problems between the order and the authorities of the church as well. Concerns such as these would consume much of Bonaventure's time and energy as minister general.

All of these movements were still living and influential elements of the world into which Bonaventure was born and in which he worked. But of even more immediate and particular concern for the understanding of his spiritual doctrine and the style of his theology in general is the shift in the locale where theology was engaged in.

It is common to think of the medieval period as a time of unexcelled peace and harmony in Christendom. But such a romanticized understanding is very misleading. The time we are concerned with, the thirteenth century, was a period of considerable turmoil concerning both the method and the content of theology. For some centuries prior to this period a style of reflection commonly described as the monastic style had come to be the familiar way of doing theology. It represented a received tradition. In that context, one knew what theology was. One knew how to go about it. And one knew where it was done and by whom. It was done in monasteries, and it was done principally by monks. It consisted, to a great extent, in prayerful reading and commentary on the Scriptures and centered largely on the daily rhythms of monastic life and liturgy. For this style of theology, the Bible was simply *the* book to be dealt with, and theology was best seen as the appropriate understanding of the Bible.

Gradually, we begin to see the emergence of a new locale for doing theology. This involved, in a first move, the creation of cathedral schools such as the well-known school of Chartres. Such schools entailed not only a shift in place from the monastery to the city but also a shift in the student body and in the choice of people who were engaged in doing theology. From the cathedral schools, the next step was the development of the medieval universities. This involved the emergence of a new professional class of scholars: theologians, who simply made a living by teaching theology at a school of the university.

As regards the style of theology, all of this meant a significant change. The monastic tradition represented a style influenced considerably by Neoplatonism, familiar with Aristotle chiefly as a grammarian. But during the late eleventh century and on into the twelfth century, matters began to change. More of Aristotle's logic came to be known. This represented a more critical approach to human knowledge and a far more systematic approach to logical argumentation, which would offer quite a different way of developing ideas and thought. As this entered into the field of theology, it led to a far more dialectical style of theological development.

Together with this, the whole of Aristotle's writings made their way into the university circles. This meant not only the logic but the physics, the metaphysics, the ethics, and so on. In summary, the philosophy of Aristotle offered an alternative worldview that was far more secular in tone than the Platonic and was at odds with the biblical and monastic theological tradition on a number of important points. Thus, both at the level of method and at the level of content, the familiar tradition was being challenged by the new movement in the universities.

How was one to react to this? By any standard, the work of

Aristotle is very impressive. To many in the thirteenth century it simply appeared to be the best that the human mind had been able to do up to that point. Should one ignore it? Or should one engage it critically? And if the latter, what shape would theology take through that engagement?

There was not a single answer to that question. But the work of Bonaventure was one attempt to deal with the issue in a creative way. Another answer to the question took the form of the extreme rationalism of the radical philosophical movement at the university level. In three sets of collations—*On the Ten Commandments, On the Gifts of the Holy Spirit,* and *On the Six Days of Creation*—we see Bonaventure as a major controversialist arguing with this crucial intellectual movement of the thirteenth century. All of these historical factors have left an impression on his thought.

Qualities of Bonaventure's Work

Against that background, I would like to suggest four qualities of Bonaventure's work that give it something of its distinctive flavor.

1. The spirit of St. Francis left an indelible impression on Bonaventure's theology. As we have seen, he was deeply influenced by friars from his earliest years. While he never would have met St. Francis personally, Bonaventure himself tells of the way he came to appreciate the Saint of Assisi at a very personal level. While he was a young boy, Bonaventure was suffering from a serious illness. In this situation, his mother prayed to St. Francis to come to the aid of her young son. In retrospect, Bonaventure writes:

When I was still a young boy, I became very seriously ill. My mother made a vow to the blessed Father Francis on my behalf, and I was pulled by him from the jaws of death and was restored to vigorous life without damage. (*LMin* [8:579])

As we have already seen, the whole of Bonaventure's education involved the influence of the friars. He developed a systematic vision deeply rooted in the spiritual experience of St. Francis, as we will see in later chapters. As general of the order, in the context of the Joachite controversies, his job was to save the order from self-destruction from within, or from possible suppression by ecclesiastical authorities. At this level, he found it necessary to confront the various interpretations of St. Francis that were operative among the friars, and to come to a personal understanding of the meaning of the Saint of Assisi.

In general we can say that he did two significant things. First, he developed a powerful theological interpretation of the person of St. Francis, which would have far-reaching effects in subsequent history. Beyond this, he developed key insights of St. Francis's spirituality into theological and metaphysical doctrines that greatly enrich the Christian tradition of theology. This had to do with a specific form of Christology, a distinctive form of trinitarian theology, and a form of creation theology that moves one strongly in the direction of a contemplative sense of the world.

2. Bonaventure's teaching, at every level, is deeply rooted in the Scriptures. This can be seen, first of all, in relation to the role of Scripture in the spirituality of Francis. In Bonaventure's *Life of St. Francis* we read:

Although he had no academic skill in the Sacred Scriptures, his untiring engagement in prayer along with his continual practise of virtue had led the man of God to such peace of mind that his intellect, illumined by the brilliance of the eternal light, penetrated the depths of Scripture with remarkable acumen. Free from every stain, his genius penetrated the hidden depths of the mysteries, and where the knowledge of the masters stands outside, the affection of the lover entered within. (*LM* 11.1 [8:535])

Concerning his own experience as a scholar, Bonaventure offers a programmatic statement early in the *Breviloquium:*

The origin of the Scriptures is not to be attributed to human research but to the divine revelation which flows from the "Father of Lights, from whom all fatherhood in heaven and on earth receives its name"; and from whom, through His Son, Jesus Christ, the Spirit flows into us. Through the Holy Spirit, who apportions His gifts and allots to everyone according as He will, faith is given; and through faith, Christ dwells in our hearts. This is the knowledge of Jesus Christ from whom the firm understanding of Scripture flows as from its origin. Therefore, no one can penetrate its meaning unless that person has first been infused with faith in Jesus Christ, for Christ is the lamp, the door, and also the foundation of the whole of Scripture. This faith is the foundation that supports us, the lamp that guides us, and the door that leads us in with respect to all supernatural illumination during our earthly sojourn, while we are exiled from the Lord. It is by this faith, moreover, that the wisdom given us by God must be measured. . . . So, it is by means of this faith that we are given the knowledge of Sacred Scripture in the measure of the blessed Trinity's outpouring. . . . (*Brevil.* prol. [5:201])

And in his *Collations on the Six Days of Creation* Bonaventure clearly states that Scripture is the first source to which the theologian must turn:

There are four kinds of books which must be approached in an orderly way. The first of these are the books of Holy Scripture. . . . The second are the original writings of the saints. . . . The third are the teachings of the Masters. The fourth are the teachings of secular teachers, that is, the doctrines of the philosophers. Anyone, therefore, who desires to learn seeks knowledge at the well-spring, that is, in Holy Scripture. For with the philosophers there is no knowledge leading to the remission of sins. Nor is there any forgiveness of sin in the Summas of the masters, since they drew from the original writings of the saints, who in turn used Scripture as their source. . . . The follower of Christ must concentrate on Sacred Scripture as children first learn their A,B,C's, and then make syllables, and then learn to read, and then finally to understand the meaning of the parts of speech. (*SD* 19.6–7 [5:421])

With this emphasis on Scripture, Bonaventure reveals his ties to the earlier monastic tradition as well as to St. Francis, who had such a profound respect for the Scriptures. Bonaventure will cite the Scriptures profusely and will expound them through the writings of the fathers, and personally through the use of both the literal and the spiritual interpretation. He himself provides a perfect synthesis of his understanding of the Scriptures in the following:

The whole of sacred Scripture teaches these three truths: namely, the eternal generation and incarnation of Christ, the pattern of human life, and the union of the soul with God. The first is concerned with faith; the second with morals; and the third with the ultimate goal of both. The effort of the doctors should be aimed at the study of the first; that of the preachers, at the study of the second; that of the contemplatives, at the study of the third. (*RA* n. 5 [5:321])

3. Next, we are dealing with a person of deep, mystical orientation. We use the word *mystical* to refer to an experience of union with God far more intense than that enjoyed in ordinary, everyday experience. This is referred to by Bonaventure as a type of experiential knowledge. What is involved with this we will discuss further in the final chapter.

St. Bonaventure was very aware of the Augustinian tradition, with its understanding of the symbolic character of creation and its exceptional emphasis on the spirituality of the inner way. He was familiar also with the Dionysian tradition with its strongly Neoplatonic overtones. This tradition, with its emphasis on the apophatic dimension of mysticism and its understanding of the threefold way of purgation, illumination, and consummation, plays a significant role in the spiritual doctrine of Bonaventure. Beyond this, Bonaventure is very familiar with the love-mysticism of the twelfth-century Victorine school, and his work shows significant influence of both Hugh and Richard of St. Victor. As we will see, all of these elements play a very noticeable role in the shaping of the Seraphic Doctor's spiritual vision.

4. Finally, Bonaventure was a highly skilled intellectual of the thirteenth century. What this meant at that time is best envisioned if we keep in mind what we have already said about the monastic style during the preceding centuries. But Bonaventure

was a theologian of the university. While his style may seem to favor the monastic style in many ways, yet it is in no way simply a continuation of that style. Far from it. If we read his early academic writings, we discover a mind that was well instructed in the style of Aristotle and fully capable of using that style should he so choose.

His conversation with Aristotle will always be critical; and his conversation with the philosophers of his own time will be even more critical. Already as a student, Bonaventure had been concerned with the rise of a philosophical movement in the context of the university. This concern would become even stronger as the years went on and the philosophers seemed to envision philosophy as a self-sufficient vision of reality. And it was a vision that differed significantly from that of the Christian religious-theological tradition. Thus, a major problem arose concerning the relation between rational knowledge and religious revelation, and between the philosophical programs developing at the universities and the work of the theologians. A text from his *Collations on the Gifts of the Holy Spirit* expresses this clearly:

There are three errors which must be avoided in the sciences. These are errors which entirely destroy the Scriptures, the Christian faith, and all wisdom. One of these is against the ground of being; another is against the ground of understanding; and the third is contrary to the order of life. The error that is against the cause of being is that concerning the eternity of the world which affirms that the world is eternal. The error against the ground of understanding is that which affirms the necessity of fate. This holds that all things happen because of necessity. The third error is that concerning the unity of the human intellect, which affirms that the intellect is one and the same in all human beings. These errors are signified in the book of the Apocalypse in the number by which the beast is named. There it is said that the beast has a name which is the number six hundred sixty-six. This is a cyclic number. Those who hold the first position base their view on the cyclical motion of time. Those who hold the second position base their view on the movement of the stars; and those who hold the third base their view on the fact that there is but one Intelligence, saying that it enters and leaves the body. This is totally false. The first error is refuted by what is written in the Old Testament: "In the beginning God created the heavens and the earth." The second error denies the importance of free will and destroys the meaning of the cross of Christ. With respect to the third, it sees no difference in merit and reward if one and the same soul is in Christ and in Judas, the traitor. The entire thing is heretical. (*GS* 8.16 [5:497–98])

What we see here is a major conflict between two worldviews. One, apparently being propagated by at least some of the philosophers and based on ancient theories of number and time, sees history as an endless, cyclic return of the same. It has no room for human freedom. In essence, it represents a very fatalistic understanding of reality. The other, based on the revelation of the Scriptures, has a richer sense of time and history, and of the importance of humans as free and ethically responsible individuals. Bonaventure can see this as serious enough that he describes the worldview of the philosophers with the apocalyptic symbol of the beast, that is, with the number 666.

When we view the work of Bonaventure against this intellectual background, we might describe it in the following way. He took the concerns of a rich tradition of spirituality and theology together with the claims of a spiritual vision grounded in the religious experience of St. Francis of Assisi and brought these into a creative engagement with some of the dominant categories of the increasingly critical and secular culture of his time.

Francis, Bonaventure, Alverna

It may seem strange to suggest that images of St. Francis might be a problem. One way to understand this is to think of the issue by way of analogy with the problems involved in the search for the historical Jesus. How much do we actually know about the figure of Jesus who walked the roads of his homeland and seemed to be busy as a wandering preacher? How does that historical information relate to the faith-confession of the early community and subsequent Christian generations? Why is it that ever since scholars began to do critical research into the historical reality of Jesus, they have come to such widely diverse conclusions? Albert Schweitzer brought his monumental study of the nineteenth-century quest for the historical Jesus to the conclusion that each author seemed to have created the Jesus that seemed most appropriate to the particular author.

Joseph Cardinal Ratzinger, in a study of Bonaventure written in 1959, made a comparison between this situation and that of St. Francis. Referring to the problem of the various biographies of Francis, he spoke of a "Francis of history" and a "Francis of faith." As there have been different understandings of the meaning and purpose of the Franciscan Order, so there have been different images of St. Francis developed to support those views.

Probably no other theologian of the order has dealt with the meaning of St. Francis as extensively as did Bonaventure. While it is true that much of Bonaventure's early experience of the order was far from Assisi in the heady atmosphere of the university town of Paris, after his appointment as minister general, he traveled to Italy to visit with the early friars who were still living, and to imbibe as much as he could of the spirit of St. Francis.

As Bonaventure reflected on all that he himself experienced on these visits, and particularly on this visit to Mount Alverna, he came to understand St. Francis as the fullest flowering of the life of the Gospel. So true did this seem that St. Francis appeared not simply as another religious founder but as a figure of truly eschatological significance. While St. Francis had called himself the herald of a great king, Bonaventure could see this as parallel to the figure of John the Baptist. Other traditions, reflected in the writings of Thomas of Celano, relate St. Francis to the prophet Elias, who must come—as Bonaventure writes—to restore all things again. A third biblical figure related to St. Francis by Bonaventure is the "angel who ascends from the rising sun." This becomes especially important in his later writings. In each of these figures we sense the seriousness with which Bonaventure deals with the evangelical perfection of St. Francis, for the main thrust of all of these is to project the image of St. Francis as a genuinely eschatological figure.

In broad terms, St. Francis is seen by Bonaventure to be a person in whom the most profound humility is but the condition for the richest inpouring of divine grace. One of Bonaventure's sermons is in essence an extended meditation on the meaning of St. Francis's humility. He writes as follows:

To be meek is to be a brother to everybody; to be humble is to be less than everybody. Therefore, to be meek and humble of heart is to be a true friar minor. (*Sermon* V [9:594])

Here we see something that had appeared already in the earlier *Disputed Questions on Evangelical Perfection,* namely, the conviction that humility is the most fundamental condition for entering on the spiritual journey. And humility involves, most basically, the awareness that deep down we are not of our own making. Each one of us is a creature brought into being by the love of God. Without that divine creative love, we would be simply and absolutely nothing. To recognize this and to see that not only are we creatures but we are fallen creatures are, at root, what Bonaventure means by the word *humility.*

In this sense, it is equivalent to poverty of spirit. And this, he argues, is true not only for members of the order but for all human beings who would enter on the journey into God.

Although it is not for everyone to take the habit and profess the Rule of the Friars Minor, it is necessary for everyone who wants to be saved to be a friar minor in the sense of being meek and humble. (*Sermon* V [9:594])

What Bonaventure sees in the Saint of Assisi is certainly exemplary for the life of all the friars. But the mystery that is lived out by St. Francis is so deeply grounded in an authentic relation to God that it is exemplary not only for the friars but for all who would be people of the Spirit. From a number of viewpoints, St. Francis is the example of one who has engaged in the spiritual journey successfully. Not only does humility define his relation to God; it comes to shape his relation to other people as well as to the entire created world. If it is true that I live and move and have my being only in the creative and salvific love of God, the same is true of all other people as well as of the entire created order.

We must then ask: What is an appropriate response to this deep truth of our being? Thus, when St. Francis comes to speak of all creatures as "brothers and sisters," this is a long way from the birdbath image through which his insights have often been trivialized.

If humility of this sort is the first step in the journey, the journey does not end there. For humility opens one to an ever deeper and fuller life of grace that will find expression in an active love and a life of virtue. If spiritual poverty is genuine, it will express itself in our relations to all things. It can eventually express itself in the form of radical voluntary poverty, and such poverty is a furnace that purifies and leads ever more deeply into conformity with the poor and naked Christ.

From the roots of humility, the human spirit grows in active love of God and neighbor which expresses itself in the virtues of the Gospel. It was this life of Christ-inspired activity that led St. Francis to a new and deeper level of spiritual experience on Alverna.

The Stigmata

It was Bonaventure's visit to Alverna that eventually led to the writing of *The Journey of the Soul into God*. But the mystery of the stigmata received by St. Francis on Alverna appears in other writings such as *The Life of St. Francis* (both the long version and the short one) and in Bonaventure's sermons, at least one of which is given over in its entirety to a discussion of the stigmatization.

Bonaventure's way of treating this aspect of St. Francis's spiritual experience reveals important insights about Bonaventure's assessment not only of St. Francis himself but also of the nature and goal of the spiritual journey. It is very clear that for Bonaventure this is the supreme experience of St. Francis. He speaks of it not only as a visionary experience but as an unusually intense ecstatic experience (see *LM* 13.1ff. [8:542]). It is here that St. Francis "became the example of perfect contemplation as he had previously been of action" (*JS* 7.3 [5:312]).

Thus, as St. Francis approached the end of his life—his death was just two years in the future—his most profound experience was of the mystical order. It now becomes clearer than ever that, for Bonaventure, the mystery of St. Francis is above all the experience of a profound spiritual journey. Never was St. Francis more a friar than on that lonely mount where, loosened from all restrictive ties to creatures, he was open to God and was so filled with the transformative power of the divine presence that it not only marked his spirit but overflowed into his flesh as well. Bonaventure writes concerning this in *The Life of St. Francis:*

Francis saw a seraph with six fiery and splendid wings descending from the highest point in the heavens. When the vision in swift flight came to rest in the air near the man of God, there appeared in the midst of the wings the image of a man crucified, with his hands and feet stretched out and nailed to a cross. Two of the wings were raised above his head and two were stretched out in flight, and two shielded his body. Seeing this, Francis was overwhelmed, and his heart was flooded with a mixture of joy and sorrow. He was overjoyed at the gracious way Christ looked upon him under the form of the seraph, but the fact that he was nailed to a cross pierced his soul with a sword of compassionate sorrow. . . . As the vision disappeared, it left his heart burning with a marvelous ardor and impressed upon his body an image of the signs which was no less marvelous. There and then the marks of nails began to appear in his hands and feet, just as he had seen them in his vision of the crucified man. (*LM* 13.3 [8:543])

To come to a deeper understanding of the mystery of Alverna, Bonaventure reaches back to the love-mysticism of the Victorines. Hugh of St. Victor had written of the power of a love-communion that transforms the lover into the likeness of the

beloved (*De arrha animae* [*Patrologia Latina* 176:954]). In his sermons about St. Francis, Bonaventure appeals to this text to shed
light on the inner dynamic of St. Francis's experience.

Hugh of St. Victor says: "So great is the power of love that it
transforms the lover into the Beloved." As the love of the Crucified was supremely and gloriously burning in his heart, so the
Crucified, in the form of the Seraph—an angelic spirit—burning
with the fire of love, appeared externally to his saintly eyes and
imprinted the sacred stigmata on his bodily members. (*Sermon
V* [9:593])

The Victorine text helps distinguish the specific form of mysticism involved in the stigmata as love-mysticism. The text helps
further to clarify the power of the symbol in which the experience of St. Francis was expressed. The transforming power of
love is symbolized by the heat of a fire that can so soften iron that
the molten material can be imprinted with any mark. The form of
the seraph evokes the same idea, for its very name—according to
Bonaventure—means a "burning love."

The way to the goal of the spiritual journey, therefore, is only
through the most burning love. But love demands a price. Insofar
as the specific object of St. Francis's reflection is the crucified
Christ, when the religious subject is bound to such an object in
the furnace of burning love, it becomes clear why at least the
spirit of St. Francis would be deeply marked by the cruciform
love of Christ. But because of the intensity of this experience, that
which marked the soul poured over into his body as well. As the
Journey of the Soul into God puts it: "his spirit shone through his
flesh"(*JS* prol. 3 [5:295]).

Viewed in this way, the stigmatization of St. Francis is a statement about the goal of the spiritual journey. Little wonder, then,
that for Bonaventure's understanding, St. Francis stands out as
the exemplar that integrates nature and grace, body and soul,
action and contemplative ecstasy. Bonaventure's understanding
of St. Francis is above all a theology of the spiritual journey,
which, within history, is oriented toward a profound, grace-filled
contemplative experience. It is on Alverna that St. Francis

embodies the *ordo seraphicus;* he has become the Seraphic Saint. (Bonaventure himself will later be known as the Seraphic Doctor.)

The six-winged seraph in the form of the Crucified will become, for Bonaventure, the symbol that brings together "six levels of illumination by which . . . the soul can pass over to peace through ecstatic elevations of Christian wisdom. There is no other path but through the burning love of the Crucified" (*JS* prol. 2 [5:295]).

These six stages of illumination will be discussed in the following chapters. It is certainly possible to argue about the intent of Bonaventure in describing these illuminations. One notices readily that, aside from the prologue (*JS* prol [5:295–96]) and the final chapter (*JS* 7.3 [5:312]) of the text, St. Francis plays virtually no role in the explanation of these illuminations.

The description of these illuminations rests on the background of works such as *The Mystical Ark* by Richard of St. Victor (also known as *Benjamin Major*). In Exodus 25, we find the elaborate description of the materials and the plan for the building of the ark the covenant. This will be used by Richard in a symbolic sense to lay out his understanding of contemplation. The theme of six levels of reflection is present already in Richard together with the two cherubs facing each other on the cover of the ark. Bonaventure will use these themes in his own structure of *The Journey of the Soul into God.*

It is possible to see the description of these illuminations as a compendium of the variety of spiritualities known in the Christian tradition. This seems to be a fair interpretation of the text of Richard of St. Victor, who, in fact, speaks of six types (*genera*) of experience. If we read the text of Bonaventure in similar terms, then the six levels of experience need not be thought of as a kind of flowchart of exercises or experiences that each person must undergo in order to arrive at the goal. Indeed, it would be very difficult to associate some of them with the personal history of St. Francis. But it is possible to see them at least as representations of different spiritualities that speak to different types of religious persons.

In this context we might think of the remarkable difference between the way of St. Francis and that of Bonaventure. That of St. Francis looks far more immediate and intuitive, uncluttered with a lot of critical questioning and philosophical analysis. That of Bonaventure is the way of an intellectual familiar with all the complexities of human consciousness and the tricks it can play. We will discuss this question further as we describe the various illuminations in the following chapters.

While the mystery of the stigmata plays such an important role in Bonaventure's understanding of the spirituality of St. Francis and provides the principal inspiration for the structure of *The Journey of the Soul into God,* there are a number of other aspects of the life of St. Francis that enter into the spirituality of Bonaventure. The understanding of God as a loving Father, which was so obvious in St. Francis's experience, will be developed by Bonaventure into a rich theology of the Trinity as the mystery of primordial love. The spirituality of the imitation of Christ will be developed into a stunning Christocentric vision of all created reality. And St. Francis's sense of the goodness and beauty of creation will be developed, by reaching back into resources in the theology of Augustine, into a powerful theology of the symbolic meaning of the cosmos.

These themes are developed extensively in Bonaventure's systematic theology. But what appears in more extended treatments at that level shimmers through unmistakably in the chapters of *The Journey of the Soul into God.* Systematic theology and spirituality are not two distinct, separated realities in the mind of Bonaventure. They clearly interact in a variety of ways.

Bonaventure's work reveals a number of important steps. First, since there were aspects of the experience of St. Francis that made it stand out as unusual in comparison with other forms of Christian spirituality, Bonaventure takes the trouble to relate that experience to the broader tradition of spirituality and biblical interpretation. We might think of the exceptional emphasis on the humanity of Jesus and particularly on the cross. But we could also think of St. Francis's relation with nature, the meaning of which would not be self-evident from the perspective of some earlier forms of Christian spirituality.

Next, Bonaventure grounds that spirituality in a metaphysical vision; eventually this involves a fully cosmic vision. We might think of this in the following way. The claims of a spirituality on one's personal life may be very far-reaching. It can become a question of fundamental importance to ask whether my personal spirituality is precisely that and nothing more. Does my personal spirituality amount to a tragic distortion of what my life could be? Or does my spirituality in fact relate me in an appropriate and life-giving way to the reality of the world of people and things in which I live, and ultimately to God? Is my spirituality really a mere psychological trick? Or is it truly life-giving and ful-filling? This will lead one eventually to ask what sort of world we live in, and how we are to relate to that world appropriately. Metaphysics is, in essence, the attempt to provide a description of the basic structures of reality. It is in the light of a good meta-physics that we may define the significance of a particular spiri-tuality.

Even a superficial reading of the Seraphic Doctor's work will make it clear that he was a thinker with an outstanding gift of synthesis. In a sense, the whole of his vision is present in each of its parts. This makes it both powerful and difficult to expound without overlapping and repetition. It might be said that for Bonaventure's way of thinking, there is no systematic theology that does not express or imply a spirituality. And there is no liv-ing spirituality that is not the concrete expression of a form of theology. What stands out in the case of Bonaventure is the fact that he was so able to give convincing expression to both the sys-tematic and the spiritual dimensions. While our presentation will focus principally on the spiritual doctrine of the Seraphic Doctor, there will be frequent pointers to the systematic theology involved with it.

As we have seen above, Bonaventure has left us with quite a collection of spiritual writings. Rather than discuss each of these works individually, our presentation will be built around the main structure of one of Bonaventure's works, *The Journey of the*

Soul into God. Over the years, particularly during the last century, it has been debated whether this is, in fact, a mystical text or whether it is best seen as a work of natural philosophy and speculative theology with a mystical intent. Without reviewing the history of this debate, we take the view that it is, indeed, a profoundly mystical text which serves to draw other levels of human intellectual and affective experience into a unified journey to the goal of mysticism. Our attempt will be to present the major themes of this particular work and to draw into that structure insights and issues from the other works of Bonaventure, both the spiritual writings and the more academic or speculative works.

All the translations provided in this volume are my own, based on the Latin edition of the Franciscans of Quaracchi. All the references are to that Latin edition and include in square brackets the volume and page numbers.

Chapter 1

Bonaventure's Program

As we have indicated above, the careful reader will find two things converging in the work of Bonaventure. One is a spiritual tradition with roots that go back clearly to St. Francis of Assisi. The other is an intellectual, theological tradition with a strong orientation to spirituality. This theological tradition has roots going back at least to the work of Augustine and includes the work of Dionysius the Areopagite, Richard of St. Victor, and Bernard of Clairvaux. The interaction between these two kinds of traditions in the context of the Aristotelian movement of Bonaventure's time gives his work something of its distinctive character and leads to a specific form of wisdom theology.

Wisdom and Knowledge

We have already spoken of the monastic tradition of theology. The writings of Bonaventure frequently show that he had considerable sympathy for that style though he was well aware of the new style that was developing in the university context. The monastic style had never been concerned with purely theoretical knowledge. It was far more concerned with opening up a vision of a way of life. In this sense, it was, for the most part, what is commonly known as a wisdom theology.

Wisdom (*sapientia*) is understood to be something more than the mere possession of knowledge (*scientia*). If we look up the word *wisdom* in the dictionary even today, we discover that it is not defined as simply the possession of a lot of information.

Rather, what is emphasized is the ability to make sound and helpful judgments concerning the relation of one's knowledge to the conduct of one's life. This may serve as a helpful entry point into the issue of wisdom in the thought world of Bonaventure.

In discussing the nature and purpose of theology in his *Commentary on the Sentences,* Bonaventure asks whether theology is purely speculative knowledge or whether it is some form of practical knowledge as well. His response demonstrates the basic qualities of a wisdom model of theology:

The knowledge presented in this book is of this sort. For this knowledge helps faith, and faith is related to the intellect in such a way that, great as it is in itself, its nature is to move the affect. And this is clear. For this knowledge that tells us that Christ has died for us, and similar things, moves a person to love unless that person is a hardened sinner. . . . Therefore, it must be conceded that we do theology so that we may become good people. (*I Sent.* prooe. q. 3, [1:13])

Speaking of wisdom in its multidimensional character, Bonaventure writes in a remarkable sermon on the mystery of the kingdom of God:

There are some dimensions of wisdom that relate to our intellect, others that relate to our desires, and others that are to be lived out. Therefore, wisdom ought to take possession of the entire person, that is with respect to the intellect, the affective life, and the person's action. (*Sermon II on the Kingdom of God* 34 [5:548])

Texts such as these indicate that the wisdom tradition as seen by Bonaventure is concerned with the process of integrating many levels of reality into a unified vision of the world and multiple levels of human experience into a unified sense of the spiritual journey of humanity. But the goal of the journey is not to be simply a knower. It is, above all, to become a lover.

To cast this in terms of our relation to God, the goal of the spiritual journey is not simply to have a conceptual knowledge about the existence and perhaps, even to some degree, about the nature of God. We are to move beyond that into a union of transforming love with the mystery of divine, creative love from which we come and to which we are called to return. "Knowledge without love is not perfect," writes Bonaventure (*I Sent.* d. 10, a. 1, q. 2, fundam. 1 [1:197]). Knowledge, then, is not the ultimate goal of the spiritual quest. But it is an element on the way.

The spiritual quest will not allow us to rest simply with knowledge. But there are those whose spiritual journey will involve extensive intellectual effort. Augustine himself is a clear case of this. His early life was an ongoing search for a God in whom he could place his faith. He was an intellectual, well trained in the disciplines of the ancient world. He bequeathed a program for Western Christianity the dynamic of which can be put very pointedly: Faith in search of understanding. One can ask questions; one can make use of all the classical disciplines to come to a deeper understanding of what it means to be a person of faith and what it is that Christians believe in. One can wish to have a deeper understanding of that which one loves.

Bonaventure comes from this tradition and carries it to one of its most powerful and coherent expressions. The wisdom tradition is not anti-intellectual. It recognizes the importance of the intellectual search for truth:

As the body without food loses its strength, beauty, and health, so the soul without the knowledge of truth becomes darkened and infirm, deformed and unstable in all things. It needs to be nourished. (*SD* 16.6 [5:410])

And the nourishment of the mind is truth. Without knowing truth, the mind may wander in strange and dangerous ways. Commenting on the inadequacy of purely theoretical knowledge, Bonaventure asks us to recall the strange situation we discover when we try to determine the precise ratio of the circumference of a circle to the diameter. The result, which still puzzles the human mind, is the strange, apparently unending chain of numbers 3.1415 . . . and so on. It is what we call *pi* in mathematics and geometry. This is a situation that has challenged mathematicians over the centuries. Bonaventure speaks about Aristotle being confronted with this strange phenomenon:

The Philosopher says it is a great pleasure to know that the diameter is asymmetrical to the circumference. Let him enjoy that if he can. (*SD* 17.7 [5:410])

About curiosity itself without a sense of reverence and piety Bonaventure reflects much of the thought of Bernard of Clairvaux when he writes:

The curious person lacks devotion. There are many such people. They are empty of praise and devotion while they are filled with the splendors of the sciences. They build wasps' nests that contain no honey, while the bees go about producing honey. (*SD* 1.8 [5:330])

In the same vein, but even more emphatically, he writes in the *Soliloquy* of the contrast between worldly wisdom and a true, authentic wisdom. The wisdom of the world is accursed, for it extinguishes the spark of the divine spirit in the human soul. By way of contrast:

If you wish to be truly wise, follow the advice of Jerome, and "learn on earth that sort of wisdom that will remain with you forever in heaven." Learn here on earth how to arrive at that One the single sight of whom leads to a knowledge of all. This is eternal truth, "without which all knowledge is ignorance, but the experience of which is perfect knowledge." (*Solil.* 2.5 [8:46])

By way of contrast with programs that are fed by *empty curiosity,* Bonaventure points to the wisdom of St. Francis:

The Blessed Francis said that he wished his friars to study provided that they would first live out what they taught. What is the point of knowing many things and tasting nothing? (*SD* 22.21 [5:440])

This highlights another aspect of the medieval understanding of wisdom. The Latin verb *sapio,* from which the noun is derived means "to taste," or "to savor." Thus, here Bonaventure can speak of tasting what one knows. As we look at his spiritual doctrine in greater detail, we will see how he speaks of internal senses with which we taste, smell, feel, and so on.

From this perspective, it becomes clear that, while Bonaventure had a great respect for the intellectual life, he did not see the pursuit of knowledge as its own end. In this area, we can feel the strong influence of such monastic authors as Bernard of Clairvaux. In his *Collations on the Gifts of the Holy Spirit,* Bonaventure quotes Bernard in the following way:

What is meant by the manner of knowing? It means to know in what order, with what desire, and for what purpose anyone should be concerned with learning: in what order, that one first learn what leads more readily to salvation; with what desire, that one might apply oneself more energetically to that learning which draws one more strongly to the love of God; for what purpose, that one might be concerned with learning not for the sake of empty glory or curiosity, but for the building up of oneself and of one's neighbor. (*GS* [5:478], quoting Bernard of Clairvaux, *Sermons on the Canticle of Canticles* 36.3)

We see here the understanding of a true intellectual reflecting on his own experience in the light of the tradition of Western wisdom theology, and in the light of the experience of St. Francis. It is in the experience of Francis that Bonaventure sees embodied most clearly what the goal of the spiritual journey is. While Francis's way to this goal was more intuitive and immediate, and not terribly complicated by intellectual questioning, the goal at which he arrived is the same goal that beckons the intellectual and all who wish to enter on the spiritual journey. The goal is that true wisdom in which the human person, by whatever way he or she may have to go because of personal characteristics, finally is drawn ever more deeply into the transforming power of the divine love in which the human spirit finally finds its light and its peace.

In the *Threefold Way,* Bonaventure provides the following overview of his vision:

For every meditation of a wise person is either about human works reflecting on what humans have done, on what they should do, and on human motivation; or this meditation is about divine works, reflecting on God's generosity to humanity because God has done all things for humanity's sake, and reflecting on how great is God's forgiveness as well as on the great things God has promised—the divine works include the mystery of creation, of reparation, and of glorification; or this meditation is about the principles behind both of the foregoing, namely God and the soul, and considers in what way they ought to be united with each other. And it is at this point that our meditation comes to rest because this is the true end of all our knowledge and activity, and this is the true wisdom in which we come to knowledge through true experience. (*TW* 1.4, 18 [8:7])

Here we see the general direction that is reflected in virtually all of Bonaventure's mystical writings. The goal is always that true wisdom which is to be found in the union between God and humanity. At times this is more implicit, lurking in the background. At other times it comes through very clearly and emphatically.

What we find in works such as the *Journey of the Soul into God* and *On the Reduction of the Arts to Theology* is a description of how this direction can be carried out by drawing all the human arts and sciences into the journey to that ultimate goal, namely, the mystical union of the person with God. It is particularly in the latter work that Bonaventure clarifies the relations of all the sciences to theology and, through theology, to mystical union:

And this is the fruit of all the sciences, that in all, faith may be strengthened, God may be honored, character may be formed, and consolation may be derived from a union of the Spouse with the beloved, a union which takes place through charity; a charity in which the whole purpose of sacred Scripture, and thus of every illumination descending from above, comes to rest—a charity without which all knowledge is vain because no one comes to the Son except through the Holy Spirit who teaches us all the truth, who is blessed forever. Amen. (*RA* n. 26 [5:325])

Here, and in the remarkable text of *The Journey of the Soul into God* we find the most synthetic statement of the Seraphic Doctor's program. It involves both the pursuit of the mind and the pursuit of the heart, both knowledge and wisdom, both the life of the intellect and the life of the mystic. It is not some sort of philosophical proof for the existence of God, since it clearly begins with a person of faith. All this is powerfully expressed in the prologue of *The Journey of the Soul into God:*

First, therefore, I invite the reader to the groans of prayer through Christ crucified . . . so that the reader will not come to believe that reading is sufficient without unction, speculation without devotion, investigation without wonder, observation without joy, work without piety, knowledge without love, understanding without humility, study without divine grace, the mirror without divinely inspired wisdom. (*JS* prol. 4 [5:296])

The head and the heart. Clearly for Bonaventure, it is not a question of choosing one to the exclusion of the other. It is, rather, a question of finding a way to unite them. We are invited to see how the pursuit of knowledge can be integrated into the total pattern of the soul's journey into God.

This does not mean that everyone must follow the intellectual way. But it does mean that the intellectual way can, indeed, be a dimension of the human journey into God for those who are personally thus inclined. But, if one uses one's head in dealing with one's religious and spiritual convictions, religion may never look precisely the same as before. Once the so-called critical moment enters into one's understanding of religion, one does not necessarily become irreligious. But one becomes a different sort of believer. A Bonaventure was not a Francis of Assisi, even though both moved to the same goal. Both were great mystics, though each followed a different road to that end.

Metaphysical Viewpoints

It is clear that for Bonaventure one of the major disputes of his time was that which revolved around the metaphysics of Aristotle. This involved, at one level, the relation of Aristotelian thought to the familiar style of Christian spirituality, which was more Platonic in orientation. At another level, it involved questions about the relation of specific Aristotelian insights to the Christian vision of the Trinity and the mystery of Christ. If Christ-centered spirituality is truly a way of entering into a saving relation with reality, what must reality look like for that to be the case?

This leads us to a number of principles of Bonaventure's thought that may seem surprising today in view of some of the contemporary critiques of religious consciousness. First, nothing that he suggests in this area is possible if a genuine religious experience is incapable of opening us to reality beyond ourselves. This runs against many modern reductionist views that tend to see religious consciousness as nothing but a form of psychological projection. That projection is involved may well be the case. That religion is nothing but projection is another question again.

A critical study of the nature of religious consciousness offers solid reason for rejecting totally reductionist theories and of giving a serious account of the significance of religious truth claims. But if religious experience can indeed open us to a dimension of transcendence beyond ourselves, then the possibility that religious experience may have metaphysical implications must be taken into account.

Related to this is the validity of the title of our present volume, which speaks of mystical writings. Over the years, the term mysticism has been defined in a variety of ways. For our purposes here, we take it to mean the conviction that it is possible for the human person to have an experience of union with God far more intense than that of ordinary human experience. Such experiences can be triggered by a wide range of realities, all of which can be thought to have mystical significance. It is clear in the case of Bonaventure that he was a person who believed that genuine mystical experiences are possible. His writings indicate some of his attempts to describe what such experiences might be, and in what circumstances they might take place.

But if the experience of Christ is taken as the foundational experience underlying the Christian tradition, this means that

Christians will discover their key insights into the meaning of humanity, the world, and God by reflecting on the mystery of Christ. Such insights, then, will function in theology in a way analogous to the role of metaphysics in philosophy. This will mean eventually that we come to relate our thought patterns to Christ in a way that corresponds to the place of Christ in creation and in human existence. In a text found in *On the Reduction of the Arts to Theology*, Bonaventure puts his vision in these terms:

In this way, understand that from the highest Mind, which is knowable to the inner senses of our mind, there has emanated from all eternity a Similitude, an Image, and an Offspring; and afterwards, when "the fulness of time came," He was united as never before to a mind and to flesh, and assumed a human form. It is through Him that all our minds are led back to God when we receive the Similitude of the Father into our hearts through faith. (*RA* 8 [5:320])

Now if the Christ-centered spiritual way of St. Francis of Assisi is an authentic religious journey, it may be taken to mean that reality as such is Christ-centered. This will become ever more clear in the writings of Bonaventure, up to and including his final work, the *Collations on the Six Days of Creation*. Probably nowhere in the history of Western Christian literature has a more consistently Christocentric vision of creation and history been formulated by anyone with the possible exception of Karl Barth or Dietrich Bonhoeffer in the twentieth century. Precisely when Bonaventure comes to see the views of certain philosophers as an attack on the intellectual center of Christendom at the University of Paris, he develops this Christocentric metaphysics, which he unfolds with a beauty and elegance reminiscent of the glorious Gothic structures in the city where he held his conferences.

Finally, it is impossible to deal with the meaning of Christ without moving to the mystery of God as Trinity. It is Bonaventure's view, therefore, that these two dogmas of Christianity—the incarnation and the Trinity—are laden with metaphysical implications that will move us beyond the philosophical visions of either Plato or Aristotle. There is a dimension to Bonaventure's theological vision that can be called a theological metaphysics, and it will function as a point of criticism for the major philosophical movements of his time.

Viewing the mystery of the Trinity in terms of the doctrine of exemplarity, Bonaventure unfolds a consistently trinitarian vision of the universe—both the universe as a whole, and each creature in the universe.

The logic of this is quite simple and direct. God is the creator of the entire universe. But God is the mystery of the Trinity. Therefore, the trinitarian God is the Creator. Bonaventure names God the *creative Trinity* (*Brevil.* 2.12 [5:230]). But if the trinitarian Creator is the exemplar, then all that comes forth in the universe in some way reflects that trinitarian exemplar. The implications of this are seen in Bonaventure's tendency to search out triadic structures and patterns at every level.

There is a text from the Gospel of John that provides significant inspiration for Bonaventure's metaphysical vision. Bonaventure has given a lengthy exposition of his understanding of the Trinity and of his conviction that the person of the Word is the central person of the Trinity. It is the Word that expresses the Father and all the things that the Father has made in creation. And it is the Word above all who leads us to union with the Father in whom all things are to be brought together. It is from this trinitarian and christological vision that Bonaventure cites the text of John 16:28:

I have come forth from the Father and have come into the world. Again I leave the world and go to the Father. (*SD* 1.17 [5:332])

Bonaventure's comment on the implication of this text is very pointed:

We could put it as follows: "Lord, I came out of You, the Supreme Being; I will return to You, and through You, the Supreme Being." (ibid.)

Then, referring back explicitly to the idea of the Word as the central person of the Trinity, he writes:

Such, then, is the metaphysical Center that leads us back, and this is the whole of our metaphysics. It deals with emanation, exemplarity, and consummation; that is, to be illumined by spiritual light and to return to the Supreme Being. And in this way you will be a true metaphysician. (ibid.)

For unless you are able to consider things in terms of how they originate, how they are brought back to their goal, and how God shines forth in them, you will have no understanding. (*SD* 3.2 [5:343])

Bonaventure had developed a strong theology of the Word as early as his youthful *Commentary on John:*

The question is asked: If the designation "Son" implies the most distinctive property, why is He here called "Word" rather than "Son"? It seems that precisely the opposite should be the case.

I respond as follows. The term "Son" expresses only the relation to the Father. But the term "Word" expresses not only the relation to the one speaking, but to that which is expressed through the word, to the sound with which it clothes itself, and to the knowledge effected in the other through the mediation of the word. And since here (in John's Prologue) the Son of God is to be described not only in terms of His relation to the Father, from whom He proceeds, but also in terms of His relation to the creatures which He has made, as well as to the flesh with which He was clothed and to the truth which He has given us, He is most nobly and fittingly described as the "Word," for that name includes all these relations, and a more fitting name could not be found anywhere in the world. (*Commentary on John* [6:247])

This text provides the program for an entire theology of revelational history, beginning with the mystery of creation, and grounds the whole in the mystery of the Trinity. God utters but one Word. It is this Word, spoken from the depths of the divine mystery, that finds expression in the world of God's creation, and in the world of salvation history and biblical revelation. It is this one Word that undergirds the whole of creation and that has become incarnate in the history of Jesus of Nazareth.

In one of his synthesizing formulations, Bonaventure speaks of the divine Word from three perspectives:

The key to contemplation is a threefold understanding: an understanding of the Uncreated Word by whom all things are produced; an understanding of the Incarnate Word by whom all things are restored; and an understanding of the Inspired Word by whom all things are revealed. For no one can have understanding without considering where things come from, how they are led back to their end, and how God shines forth in them. (*SD* 3.2 [5:343])

Christ is, for Bonaventure, the preeminent embodiment of divine Wisdom. He is, in the fullest sense of the word: "the way, and the truth, and the life" (John 14:6). Any other claim to wisdom must be brought into relation with this wisdom. Philosophy, then, which at the level of Aristotle's understanding of metaphysics is a search for the ultimate principles of reality, is best seen not as a self-sufficient form of human knowledge but as a stage in the larger pattern of the spiritual journey of humanity into God.

But that journey, which in the case of St. Francis was uncomplicated by extensive rational inquiry, takes a different form in the life of the intellectual scholar. In the latter case, rational philosophy is seen as a necessary and important development of the human mind. But it cannot be allowed to rest in itself. The intellectual person is to move through the process of rational inquiry in philosophy, and even in theology, only to culminate in a form of ecstatic, transforming love of the divine in which the human person is drawn beyond the categories of rational discourse ever deeper into a mystery that it never comprehends. To make philosophy, or any other cognitive discipline, an end in itself, therefore, is to abort a process in a way that allows a part to be taken for the whole and to be seen as self-contained or self-sufficient.

This means that, for Bonaventure, all the arts and sciences together with philosophy can play an important role in the journey of the soul, at least for people who are intellectually inclined. But clearly, for Bonaventure, all these human cognitive endeavors must be left open to the insights gained from the historical experience of the biblical revelation and, specifically, the historical experience of Jesus Christ as this is reflected on in the history of the Christian community.

Inspired as he is by the tradition of Augustine, Bonaventure is concerned with the ideal of the unity of Christian wisdom. At the basic level of methodology, this means that we must take into account the possibility that, as we have seen above, the answer to some of the most basic philosophical questions might be discovered not in philosophical reflection that abstracts from Christianity but precisely from the historical, religious experience that provides the basic clues to Christian self-understanding.

The implications of this can be seen at a number of crucial points in the writings of Bonaventure. The above citation from the *Collations on the Six Days of Creation* is one of the clearest statements of it. The same idea appears elsewhere in the form of a prayer:

It is proper at the beginning of any good work to call upon the One from Whom all good things proceed as from their source, by Whom they are produced as by their Exemplar, and to Whom they return as to their end. This is the ineffable Trinity: Father, Son, and Holy Spirit. (*Solil.* prol. [8:28])

In summary form, this means that all of creation is on a journey. All pours out from the Father through the mediation of the Word and is brought to full fruition in the power of the Spirit. As it is the Word through whom all pours forth from God, so it is the Word who leads us to union with the Father in whom all creation will eventually converge. The work of the Spirit is to bring us ever more into the mystery of the Word who has been manifested to us most explicitly in the form of the incarnation. In the incarnation, the center of God becomes present as the center of creation.

In this sense, He is the *Tree of Life,* for by means of this center we return to the very fountain of life and are revived in it. (*SD* 1.17 [5:332])

From this perspective, the point of the spiritual journey is to become personally aligned with the mystery of the Word so that as consciously knowing and loving creatures, human beings enter into the Word's relation with the Father and the Spirit. This is to be realized expressly in human life. But it is through humanity that the destiny of the rest of the cosmos will be brought to realization.

Point of Departure for the Journey

Early in *The Journey of the Soul into God* Bonaventure presents three themes that are important for understanding the point of departure for the spiritual journey. The prologue gives eloquent testimony that Bonaventure is engaged in a search for peace. It also sees the person who engages in this journey to be a person of desire. A title found immediately before the beginning of the first chapter reads: "Here starts the speculation of the poor one in the desert" (*JS* 1.1 [5:296]). A few comments on each of these will help set the stage for the journey.

Concerning the theme of peace, Bonaventure had been involved for two years in trying to heal the divisions that had been tearing the Franciscan Order apart. This meant considerable travel and consultation with the friars. He went to Assisi itself to talk with those who had the strongest living memories of St. Francis. Then he visited Mount Alverna. He described his visit there in the following words:

Following the example of the most blessed father, Francis, I came with a yearning spirit searching for that peace; I, a sinner, who—though completely unworthy—succeeded as the seventh minister general of the brothers in place of that same most blessed Father after his death.... Moved by divine inspiration, I withdrew to Mount Alverna, to that place of quiet, to satisfy the search of my soul for peace. (*JS* prol.1–2 [5:295])

It was while there that Bonaventure came to his insights concerning the meaning of the experience of St. Francis that would eventually be put into writing in the form of *The Journey of the Soul into God.*

The prologue uses the figure of the prophet Daniel to describe the person who wishes to embark on the journey. Daniel is described by Bonaventure as a person of desires.

For no person is disposed in any way for those divine contemplations which lead to spiritual ecstasy except one who, like Daniel, is a "person of desires." Such desires are aroused in us in two ways, namely, through the cry of prayer which leads us to groan from anguish of heart; and through the light of speculation, by which the mind turns most directly and intensely to the rays of light. (*JS* prol. 3 [5:296])

Neutrality will not work in this journey. A person must deeply desire union with the divine. This desire will manifest itself in deep and constant prayer. Prayer, for its part, will help open the human person to be receptive to the utterly free grace of God. And without the aid of divine grace, the mystical journey cannot be carried out successfully.

No matter how the interior stages may be ordered, nothing will happen unless the divine aid accompanies us. But this divine aid comes to all who seek it with a truly humble and devout heart. And this means to truly sigh for divine aid in fervent prayer in this vale of tears. Prayer, therefore, is the mother and source of every upward striving of the soul. Thus, Dionysius, in his book *Mystical Theology,* wishing to instruct us concerning ecstasies of the soul, places a prayer at the beginning. Let us, therefore, pray, and let us say to the Lord, our God: "Lead me, O Lord, in your way, and I will enter into your truth. Let my heart rejoice that it may fear your name." (*JS* 1.1 [5:297])

Concerning the nature and importance of prayer for the journey, Bonaventure writes to women religious in the small work *On the Perfection of Life:*

Prayer is a vessel by which the grace of the Holy Spirit is drawn from that font overflowing with sweetness, the most blessed Trinity. . . . Have I not already explained to you what prayer is? Listen again. Prayer is the turning of the mind toward God. Do you wish to know how you ought to turn your mind toward God? Pay attention. When you pray, you ought to gather up your entire self, enter with your Beloved into the chamber of your heart, and remain there alone with Him, forgetting all external affairs; and so you should elevate yourself with all your heart and all your mind, and with all your affection, desire, and devotion. And you should not let your mind wander away from your prayer, but as long as you can, rise up by the fervor of your devotion until you enter into the "place of the wonderful tabernacle, even to the house of God." There the eye of your heart will be delighted at the sight of your Beloved, and you will "taste and see how good the Lord is," and "how great is His goodness." Then you will rush into His embraces. You will kiss Him with such intimate devotion that you will be completely carried away, wholly enraptured in heaven, totally transformed into Christ. You will not be able to contain your spirit, but will cry out with the prophet David: "My soul refused to be comforted: I remembered God, and was delighted." (*PL* 5.5 [8:119])

Keeping all this in mind, we understand why it is that Bonaventure urges his readers to move slowly through the text and reflect prayerfully on the thoughts and issues that it deals with. He does not want the reader to think:

that mere reading will be enough without unction, speculation without devotion, investigation without wonder, observation without exultation, hard work without piety, knowledge without love, understanding without humility, study without divine grace, the mirror without divinely inspired wisdom. (*JS* prol. 4 [5:297])

The necessity of desire in the spiritual journey remains in Bonaventure's writings until his final work, where he says:

The door to wisdom is a yearning for it and a powerful desire. Therefore the Psalm says: "Open wide your mouth and I will fill it." That is the road by which wisdom comes to me; by which I enter into wisdom, and wisdom enters into me. The same is true of charity. Hence, "God is love, and those who abide in love abide in God and God in them." Such wisdom cannot be obtained without supreme mutual pleasure; but where one looks for supreme mutual pleasure, supreme desire must be there first. (*SD* 2.2 [5:336])

Later in the same work he writes concerning the soul and the illuminations coming from God:

For the soul to receive these illuminations, a lively desire is required, together with clear scrutiny and tranquil judgment. For there is no contemplative soul without a lively desire. One who does not have this knows nothing of contemplation, because the origin of the illuminations goes from the highest to the lowest, and not the reverse. (*SD* 22.29 [5:441–42])

The "poor one in the desert." This phrase elicits a number of thoughts. The most obvious possibility is that it is a reference to the fact that Bonaventure is a mendicant and is a poor one in that sense. But that can be related to yet another level of meaning. The poor one is one who recognizes precisely what he or she is before God: a creature, and a fallen creature. These two elements, as we have seen above, constitute the core of what Bonaventure understands as spiritual poverty. And without such spiritual poverty, there can be no deep desire for the fulfilling relation with God that is the concern of the journey. In view of that, the spiritual journey as here conceived is simply impossible without the recognition of one's poverty before God.

Bonaventure places the poor one "in the desert." This phrase recalls the tradition of the desert as a place of testing and a place of encounter with the divine. The wandering of the Hebrew people for forty years in the desert comes to mind as an obvious biblical example. And a later prophet, Hosea, describes God as a lover who will lead the unfaithful spouse back to the desert to win her heart once again. Together with the theme of testing, the desert is known in spiritual traditions as a place of encounter with the divine. Such a combination of themes is clearly connected with the need for conversion from human sinfulness and with asceticism.

We need to know that there are three things in us the use of which will enable us to proceed in this triple way: the sting of conscience, the ray of intelligence, and the little flame of wisdom. If you wish to be cleansed, turn to the sting of conscience; if you wish to be enlightened, turn to the ray of intelligence; if you wish to reach perfection, turn to the little flame of wisdom. (*TW* 1.2 [8:3])

What follows from this is a detailed description of how one ought to call to mind one's sins and failings, how one ought to feel sorrow for them and pray for forgiveness. It is an unrelenting call to the awareness of one's negligence and sinfulness and a call to attentive prayer to move beyond such weaknesses.

The entire context leaves no doubt as to what Bonaventure has in mind. He will lead us on a profound contemplative journey. The goal is a deep, personal union with God. Over and over again, he will lead us to an encounter with our world, with ourselves, and with God. The way to that goal will take us through the mysteries of God's creation. But, in order that we do not become hopelessly enmeshed in created things, the practice of asceticism becomes necessary so that we can realize in ourselves the necessary inner, spiritual freedom.

But how is the world shaped, and how is human nature equipped for this journey? Concerning the world, the metaphysical structure we have already described is basic: emanation, exemplarity, and consummation. All pours forth from the mystery of divine, creative love; all is shaped in some similarity to the divine Archetype; and all is to move back into unity with the loving from which the river of creation emanates.

Viewed from another perspective, Bonaventure, following the Victorine insights, distinguishes a world outside ourselves, a world within ourselves, and a world above ourselves. The first is clearly the world of bodily beings that can be experienced empirically. The second is the world of spiritual reality such as we discover within the human person and the human soul. The third has to do with the mystery of the divine, which transcends anything at either of these levels.

Concerning the equipment of the human person for this journey in this three-leveled reality, Bonaventure's description of this amounts to an outline of the journey itself:

[O]ur mind has three principal ways of perceiving. The first way refers to corporeal things outside the soul, and this is called animality or sensitivity. The second way looks inward within itself, and this is called spirit. The third way involves looking above itself, and this is called mind. With all of these we should be disposed to ascend to God, so as to love God with all our heart, with all our soul, and with all our mind. In this consists the perfect observance of the Law and, at the same time, Christian wisdom. (*JS* 1.4 [5:297])

This reflects the classical Christian outline of the spiritual way going back at least to Augustine. In his final work, Bonaventure explicitly traces his treatment of this to Gregory the Great. He refers it also to a certain philosopher who, in this case, is probably not Aristotle but the author of the *Book of Causes:*

The third way of distinguishing within the soul in relation to the return to God follows three levels of contemplation. Gregory, commenting on Ezechiel, sets up three levels: whatever becomes an object of our consideration is either outside us, inside us, or above us. Therefore, God is contemplated in those things that are inside us, outside us, or above us, by means of three powers, the exterior, the interior, and the superior, that is the apprehensive, the affective, and the operative. And according to a philosopher, "every noble soul has three operations," that is, the animal toward things outside, the intellectual toward things inside; and the divine toward things above. (*SD* 22.34 [5:442])

In this view, one moves "from that which exists outside us" to "that which exists inside us" to "that which exists above us." Then, playing with the symbolic significance of the number six, which stands out so strongly in the biblical tradition, and drawing, no doubt, on the *Mystical Ark* of Richard of St. Victor, Bonaventure proceeds to show in what sense there are six steps involved in this ascent to God: two involved in reflection on the world outside ourselves, two involved in reflection on the world within ourselves, and two involved in reflection on the mystery of God. He then goes on to show how the human person is equipped with six powers corresponding to these six levels:

In accordance with the six stages of the ascent to God, there are six levels in the powers of the soul by which we ascend from the lowest to the highest, from things external to things internal, from temporal things to eternal things. These are: sense, imagination, reason, intellect, intelligence, and high point of the mind or the spark of synderesis. These grades we have implanted in us by nature. They have been deformed through sin, and have been reformed by means of grace. They must be cleansed by justice, exercised by knowledge, and perfected by wisdom. (*JS* 1.6 [5:297])

This doctrine of the six levels of reflection corresponding to six powers of the soul can be traced to a text mistakenly attributed to Augustine, *On the Spirit and the Soul.* This material can be found in Isaac of Stella as well and can be traced back to Boethius and Augustine. These six powers should be understood not as faculties of the soul but as functions of the soul.

The concern with the high point of the mind, *apex mentis,* corresponds to the interior point of integration of the many diverse functions and faculties of the soul. If we follow the inner way, our tendency will be to speak of this point in the language of depth. But if we follow the lead of Augustine, we recognize that the depth of our interiority is identical with the high point. The turn inward is simultaneously the turn upward. Thus, for Bonaventure, the term points to that inner point of wholeness and integration which is crucial for the mystical experience. Commenting on the return of the Magi to their homeland, he writes:

The fifth day of their return takes place by means of the recollection of the soul.... The soul which has been spread out through imaginings, thoughts, affections, and speech should now be gathered in.... There are seven interior powers, like a circle within a circle, which need to be gathered together, namely sense, imagination, estimation, which is midway between reason and the imagination because it apprehends something of the spiritual good; reason, through which the soul knows itself, and in knowing itself, knows other spiritual substances; the intellect, in which the principles of the eternal laws abide; intelligence, which contemplates God Himself; and the apex of the mind, which is the very height of the soul, and is, as it were, the center in which all the other powers are gathered together. (*Sermon 4 on Epiphany* [9:162])

In *The Journey of the Soul into God,* from a different perspective, Bonaventure addresses the same issue:

Those who wish to ascend to God must avoid sin which deforms nature. They must exercise the above-mentioned natural powers by prayer to receive regenerating grace; by a good life to receive purifying justice; by meditation to receive the illumination of knowledge; and by contemplation to receive the wisdom that perfects. Just as grace is the foundation of the will's rectitude and of the penetrating enlightenment of reason, so first we must pray; second, we must live in a holy manner; third, we must concentrate on the reflections of truth and, by concentrating on these, mount step by step until we come "to the high mountain" where we shall see the "God of gods in Sion." (*JS* 1.8 [5:298])

With this we gain a sense of the six stages in the structure of the journey and the relation of these steps to an understanding of the human subject who is to undertake it. It is a person of faith who engages in this journey. Therefore it would be a mistake to think of this as some sort of proof for the existence of God. It is from the standpoint of faith that one looks at reality to discern its deepest message.

We will try to follow this way with the Seraphic Doctor in the spirit which he himself suggests, a spirit of prayer and meditation embracing both our head and our heart, both our intellect and our affect, seeking to find that sense of integration and wholeness in which peace is to be found. We will move from the "outside world" to the "inside world" to the "mystery above ourselves," looking at each level from two perspectives until all converge in the mystery of Christ. At that point, Bonaventure invites us to move with and through Christ into the silence of loving, mystical union.

Chapter 2

The World Outside

The first chapter of *The Journey of the Soul into God* introduces the reader to a way of reflecting on the mystery of the created order. Here the experience of St. Francis interacts with the theological and philosophical reflection of Bonaventure in a fascinating way. We are concerned above all with the sense of the familial unity of the entire created order that appears in the life of St. Francis, and with the way in which Bonaventure reflects on this in terms of theology and spirituality.

It is very obvious that this view of the material universe differs greatly from that of the medieval vision of Catharism, with its conviction that material reality is fundamentally evil. But beyond this it has been argued that the vision of St. Francis involves a spirituality that places a distinctive emphasis on the material world. In the case of Francis, and in the Bonaventurean development of the vision of Francis, the material world of God's creation plays a very positive role in spirituality. That the world can be a problem, even for Bonaventure, we will see later. But that is no longer a case of the world precisely in its material nature as God's creation. It is quite a different question.

What we find in Bonaventure, first of all, is a spirituality that sees a very positive, spiritual significance in material beings and in human sense experience. Those who are familiar with the writings of the ancient Eastern Christian writers such as Origen, Clement of Alexandria, and Maximus the Confessor will notice striking affinities between their sense of cosmic mysticism and that of Bonaventure.

The Experience of St. Francis

Before looking directly at Bonaventure's reflections on the external world of creation, it might be helpful to recall something of the life of St. Francis. Of basic significance is the scene before the bishop of Assisi early in the process of the saint's conversion. It will be recalled that Francis had come into considerable conflict with his biological father, Pietro Bernardone, because of the way the son was using or giving away the goods of his father to the needy who appealed for help. In a desperate effort to resolve the conflict, the two appeared before the bishop seeking his mediation and judgment. It is there, in a scene laden with drama, that Francis stripped off all his clothing and returned everything to his father saying:

Until now I have called you father here on earth, but now I can say without reservation, "Our Father who are in heaven," since now I place all my treasure and all the confidence of my hope in him. (*LM* 2.4 [8:508])

The deep sense of God as loving source of all, on whom Francis is now totally dependent stands out strongly. Surely it is a long way from the scene before the bishop to the composition of the *Canticle of Creatures* toward the end of his life. But the idea that appears in the *Canticle* of a universal familial relation uniting all creation is not new. It has been with St. Francis all along ever since this scene with his father, but it is radicalized in the *Canticle* as his personal experience of reconciliation with what has been happening to him is translated into a sense of reconciliation with all aspects of creation.

From this perspective, we can begin to understand why it is that in the mind of Francis, radical poverty as a spiritual outlook assumes such foundational importance. One does not divide up and carry home as private property what is God's common gift to all. If I sit near a great waterfall with no concern for owning it or using it to generate power or keeping other people away from it, then I am truly free to see it and to enjoy it as a reflection of nature's beauty. I can rejoice in it. I do not need to be tied to it by ownership. This might give at least some insight into the connection between a deep creation theology and the meaning of spiritual poverty. Such a spiritual outlook makes room for a deeper sense of our bonds to all other creatures in the world of God's creation.

The early biographies of St. Francis are consistent in describing this sort of relation between the "Little Poor Man" and the created world. Because he chose to possess nothing, in a sense, all things were his to enjoy. As Thomas of Celano writes:

> He praised the Artist in every work of the artist. . . . He rejoiced in all the works of the Lord's hands, and behind all things that were pleasant to behold he saw their life-giving reason and cause. In beautiful things he saw Beauty itself; all things were good to him. "He who made us is the highest Good," they cried out to him. . . . From all things he made a ladder for himself by which he could come even to His throne. (See Celano, *Legenda* 2.124, 165)

Bonaventure writes in similar terms in *The Life of St. Francis:*

> In everything beautiful, he saw Beauty itself. . . . With the power of an unusual devotion, he savored in each and every creature that fontal Goodness flowing in them as in so many small streams. And he perceived a divine harmony in the interplay of powers and activities God has given them. And like the prophet David, he sweetly exhorted them to praise the Lord. (*LM* 9.1 [8:530])

In brief, St. Francis is seen by his early biographers as a person who had an exceptional ability to discover the traces of God in the world of nature. He was a man possessed of an extraordinary love for created things. For him the whole of creation is a gift from God and a sacramental manifestation of God. The entire created order could well be seen as a family because all creatures have their origin in God. This is what all things share in common.

Bonaventure's Development

Bonaventure takes up St. Francis's vision of creation and enriches it by relating it to some of the great philosophical insights that have helped him in to define their place in the world. Bonaventure agrees with Celano that what is distinctive about St. Francis's vision of creation is his feeling of belonging to one and the same family with all other creatures. Bonaventure writes:

> When he considered the source of all things, he was filled with even greater piety, calling creatures—no matter how small—by the name of brother or sister, because he knew they had the same source as himself. (*LM* 8.6 [8:527])

The Objective World of Creation

As we have indicated already, St. Francis can be seen as a person of immediate religious experience. On the other hand, Bonaventure appears as the theologian who, more completely than any other, transformed this religious experience into a rich theological vision of creatures as mirrors reflecting God's power, wisdom, and goodness. We can single out three interrelated points that illustrate this.

First, the *loving Father* of St. Francis becomes the theological mystery of primal Goodness, the principle of fontal fullness in which is grounded the mystery of the divine persons within the Trinity, and the circle of creation that flows like a river outside the Trinity. Details of Bonaventure's theology of the Trinity will be discussed in a later chapter. For now, it is sufficient to point out that trinitarian theology provides a rich background to the simple, direct confession of St. Francis concerning God as universal Father.

Corresponding to Bonaventure's understanding of the triune, creative God, the entire cosmos can be seen as a vast symbol of God. At this point, Bonaventure reveals clear traces of Augustine's theology of creation. It is here that Bonaventure works with a well-developed theology of *exemplarity*.

One might envision God as an artist. As a human artist has an idea in his or her mind and tries to render that idea externally in some object of art such as a statue, a painting, or a work of music or literature, so God has an Idea in mind and projects that Idea externally to bring forth the created universe. The universe, therefore, can be seen as a work of art that expresses the divine Idea in something that is not God; that is, the created universe.

> So it appears that the entire world is like a single mirror, full of lights that stand in the presence of the divine Wisdom, shedding light like burning coals. (*SD* 2.27 [5:340])

All creatures reflect God in some way, even though it may be a very distant reflection. In this sense, everything in the created order may be seen at least as a vestige of its divine, creative source. The Latin word for vestige means simply a footprint. A vestige, in Bonaventure's usage, may be compared with the footprint of a person in the sand of the beach. One who discovers the footprint may not discover a lot about the person who left it there. But something can be known about the person's size, weight, and so on. So it is with the relation of all creation to God. Every created reality can open us to some awareness of the source of this footprint. But at best it is a distant and unclear knowledge.

Within this cosmos, all of which reflects God in some way, there is a particularly intense reflection to be found in the human creature. Humanity is to reflect God with a particular responsibility. It is not simply a vestige. It is an *image* of the divine. Its task is, above all, to bring to conscious expression the song of creation, which Augustine described centuries earlier: "We did not make ourselves, but we were made by God who is forever" (*Confessions* bk. 9, 10, 25). It is in humanity that this song of creation finds conscious voice. As Bonaventure writes:

> In all of us there arises a praise of God in all things. All creatures cry out: "God." What, then, should I do? I will sing out together with them. The thick string on the zither does not sound pleasant by itself. But in harmony with others it does. (*SD* 18.25 [5:418])

Francis's sense of familial relations among creatures plays a crucial role in Bonaventure's understanding of the spirituality of St. Francis. The inner dynamism of such a vision must lie in the shaping of all our relations to reality in the light of the mystery of the divine, creative love. If God so loves the world and all in it, how can we not love the world of God's creation. It is, indeed, the creative love of God confessed by St. Francis in the scene before the bishop that flows out into all the elements of creation so that our Creator-God is simultaneously the creator of the entire universe. And the plan for reflecting on God's creation is laid out before us:

In this sort of prayer one is enlightened to know the steps of the ascent to God. For we are created in such a way that the universe itself is a ladder for ascending to God. And among creatures, some are vestiges and others are images; some are corporal, and others are spiritual; some are temporal, and others are everlasting; some are outside of us, others are inside us. So that we might arrive at the first Principle which is most spiritual and eternal and above us, we must pass through those vestiges which are corporal and temporal and outside us. And this is what it means to be led in the way of God. Next we must enter into our mind, which is the image of God, an image which is everlasting, spiritual, and within us; and this is to enter into the truth of God. Then we must transcend ourselves to that which is eternal, most spiritual, and above us by looking at the First Principle. And this is what it means to rejoice in the knowledge of God and in reverence for God's majesty. (*JS* 1.2 [5:297])

Though Bonaventure uses many symbols to elicit a sense of the religious meaning of the created world, two of his favorite symbols are that of the book and that of the window. The entire universe can be thought of as a book. Here we are dealing with a metaphor drawn from the human experience of knowledge and language.

Human knowledge is internal to the mind of the knower. When a person wishes to express that knowledge to another, it takes the external form of sound; the sound of the human voice shaping words that symbolize the thoughts that remain in the speaker's mind. Knowledge takes the form of language and can be communicated in the form of speech and writing. A written document, therefore, is the external, symbolic expression of the internal knowledge in the mind of the author.

When applied to God and to creation, this suggests that God's inner Word of knowledge becomes the cosmos when it is projected outward. The cosmos, then, is comparable to a language system, or a book. The inner content of this book is the eternal Word of God. In learning how to read this cosmic book, therefore, we are learning something about God. Without doubt, if Bonaventure were to pick up the writings of some twentieth-century cosmologists and discover how they speak of their work as "reading the mind of God," he would no doubt resonate with the language, though he would have a fundamentally different understanding of what the language means.

The entire world is, as it were, a kind of book in which the Creator can be known in terms of power, wisdom, and goodness which shine through in creatures. (*Commentary on Wisdom* 13.5 [6:193])

Because our human vision has become distorted through the influence of sin, however, we find it difficult to read this book correctly. It has become for us almost an "unknown language—like Hebrew or Greek—and the book of the universe has become unknown to us" (*SD* 2.20 [5:340]).

Therefore, we need the help of another book to enable us to read the book of creation. If sin has blinded us to the mystery of the cosmos, the gift of God's grace will again open our eyes, and with the help of a second book, the Sacred Scriptures, we will learn again to read the book of creation. And the central point of both the cosmic and the scriptural books is compacted into the mystery of Christ; for, in his humanity, Christ can be described as an external book in which the internal book of God's Word becomes incarnate in the most intense and explicit way. Speaking about the book of creation from the perspective of the original creation and the Fall, Bonaventure writes:

It is certain that as long as humanity stood upright, humans possessed the knowledge of created things and through their significance, they were carried up to God; to praise, worship, and love God. This is the purpose of creation, and this is how creation is led back to God. But after the Fall, this knowledge was lost, and there was no longer anyone to lead creatures back to God. Therefore, this book—the world—became dead and illegible. And another book was needed through which this one would be lighted up, so that it could receive the symbolic meaning of created things. This book is the book of Scripture which establishes the likenesses, the properties, and the symbolic meaning of those things written down in the book of the world. And so, Scripture has the power to restore the entire world and bring it to the knowledge, praise, and love of God. (*SD* 13.12 [5:390])

The deep meaning of the book of the world and the book of Scripture is expressed in its most compact form in the mystery of the incarnation of the Word:

The one who was invisible in the first instance became visible for our sake. Now as a mental word cannot be heard before it is expressed vocally, but becomes audible to us when it has been clothed with the sound of the voice, so the Incarnate Word, before His birth, could not be understood. But after His birth, when He had clothed Himself with flesh just as a word is expressed by the voice, He became perceptible to us. So it is that Augustine writes in *De doctrina christiana* 1, "Just as when we speak so that what we have in our mind may enter into the mind of the hearer through the ears of the flesh, and the word that we carry in our heart becomes a sound which is called speech, and yet our thought is not changed into sound but remains integral in itself even while assuming the form of sound by which it can impinge on the ears without any mark of change in itself, so the Word of God was made flesh that He might dwell among us while undergoing no change in Himself." The Word became not only audible but visible as well. In itself, it is more fitting that a word be heard than that it be seen. But the Word of the Father, which could be neither heard nor seen, became both visible and audible in His birth. So it is that 1 John 1 writes:

> This is what we proclaim to you:
> what was from the beginning,
> what we have heard,
> what we have seen with our eyes,
> what we have looked upon,
> and our hands have touched—
> we speak of the Word of Life.
> This Life became visible.
> We have seen and bear witness to it,
> and we proclaim to you the eternal Life
> that was present to the Father
> and became visible to us.
> (*Sermon 1 on the Nativity of the Lord* [9:103])

Thus, by means of the single metaphor of the book with its full linguistic background, the Seraphic Doctor draws together in a powerful way the mystery of creation with that of incarnation.

As regards the symbol of "window," we need to think of the glorious stained glass going into two magnificent Gothic structures in the city of Paris during the lifetime of Bonaventure: the cathedral of Notre Dame and the remarkable Saint Chapelle. Both of these buildings present the visitor, even today, with an orgy of richly colored light, broken into patterns of the most varied hues, the color-tones shifting as the sun moves around the exterior of the buildings. Both are situated in the center of Paris, where Bonaventure delivered the following statement in 1273, a text that combines the metaphor of the book with that of the window:

The entire world is a shadow, a road, a vestige, and it is also a book written outside (of God). For in each creature there is a shining forth of the divine exemplar, but mixed with darkness. Hence creatures are like a kind of darkness mixed with light. Also in every creature there is a road leading to the exemplar. Just as you see that a ray of light entering through a window is colored in different ways according to the different colors of the various parts, so the divine ray shines forth in each and every creature in different ways and in different properties. It says in Wisdom: "Wisdom shows herself in her ways." So, the

creature is a vestige of the wisdom of God. Therefore, the creature is nothing other than a certain likeness of the divine wisdom; a kind of statue. For all these reasons, creation is a
certain book written outside. (*SD* 12.14 [5:386])

In *The Journey of the Soul into God,* Bonaventure writes:

Creatures are shadows, echoes, and pictures of that most powerful, most wise, and most perfect Principle. . . . They are vestiges, representations, spectacles proposed to us and signs
divinely given so that we can see God. These creatures are . . .
exemplifications presented to souls still untrained and immersed
in sensible things so that through the sensible things they see,
they will be led to intelligible things which they do not see as
through signs to that which is signified. (*JS* 2.11 [5:302])

To the degree that our souls are cleansed of sin by grace and
our spiritual senses again come to function in a healthy way, the
whole of the cosmos can be seen to reflect something of the richness of the divine life.

The supreme power, wisdom, and benevolence of the Creator
shine forth in created things insofar as the bodily senses make
them known to the interior senses in three ways. For the bodily senses serve the intellect when it investigates rationally, or
believes faithfully, or contemplates intellectually. One who contemplates considers the actual existence of things; one who
believes considers the habitual course of things; and one who
investigates with reason considers the potential excellence of
things. (*JS* 1.10 [5:298])

After drawing the reader through a series of triadic structures
in relation to each of the above-mentioned functions of the soul,
Bonaventure concludes:

Therefore, from visible things, the soul rises to reflect on the
power, wisdom, and goodness of God insofar as God exists,
lives, and is intelligent, purely spiritual and incorruptible and
immutable. (*JS* 1.13 [5:299])

Discovering God in Sense Experience Itself

From here, the next level of Bonaventure's reflection is concerned with how to read the book of the cosmos not in its objective existence outside the mind but in the actual human sense experience of the cosmos. The theological principle that stands in the background is that God is present in all creatures by reason of the divine essence, power, and presence (*JS* 2.1 [5:299]).

At this level of reflection, it is a question of what goes on in our bodies when the external world of empirical realities impinges on human experience through our sense organs. In terms characteristic of the medieval understanding of human nature (microcosm) and its relation to the physical universe (macrocosm), Bonaventure writes:

It should be noted that this world, which is called the macrocosm, enters our soul, the microcosm, through the doors of the five senses in as far as sense objects are experienced, enjoyed, and judged. (*JS* 2.2 [5:300])

In discussing these three functions—experience, enjoyment, and judgment—involved in the process of sensation, Bonaventure leads the reader from the point at which the external data impinge on the sense organs to reflect on the way in which sense pleasure arises at the level of sensation. This involves qualities such as beauty, sweetness, or wholesomeness. At this level, Bonaventure offers reflections on the nature of beauty which he describes in terms that hark back to Pythagorean mathematics and ancient Greek aesthetics together with the philosophical principle that virtue lies in the middle between the extremes:

"Beauty is nothing other than numerical proportion," or a "certain disposition of parts together with pleasing color." Again proportion, in as far as it involves power or strength, is called pleasure when the power acting does not disproportionately exceed the sense organ receiving it. For the senses are pained by extremes and delighted by moderation. . . . Thus through pleasure, delightful external objects enter the soul by means of their likeness to produce three kinds of pleasure. (*JS* 2.5 [5:301])

From this follows the judgment that this is indeed a beautiful or delightful object. And it is because of its beauty that it evokes an experience of delight in the human person. Here in the judgment the triadic structure of sensation is completed. And already here in this triadic structure (experience, enjoyment, judgment) involved in sense experience, Bonaventure sees a vestige of the Trinity. The issue of aesthetics is drawn out yet further:

Since all things are beautiful and in some way delightful, and since beauty and delight do not exist without proportion, and since proportion is found primarily in numbers, all things must involve number. Therefore, "number is the principal exemplar in the mind of the Creator," and in things it is the principal vestige leading to Wisdom. Since this is most evident to all and very close to God, it leads us ... very close to God. It makes God known in all bodily and sensible things when we perceive them in terms of number, when we take delight in their numerical proportions, and when we make definite judgments in accordance with the laws of numbers. (*JS* 2.10 [5:302])

God is seen here as the basic principle that undergirds any true and solid human judgment about the beauty of creation. The laws or standards—or the judicial numbers, as Augustine referred to them—preexist creation in the eternal Word of God, or in the divine Art. The deepest truth about creatures is not to be found in the simple fact of their physical existence or in our knowledge of their chemical makeup. It is found, rather, in the awareness that each creature is a symbol pointing beyond itself to the eternal Archetype. From this we can conclude that it is possible: "that all creatures in this sensible world lead the spirit of the contemplative and the wise person to the eternal God" (*JS* 2.11 [5:302]).

Without doubt, any object in the world around us can be of significance in our search for the mystery of God. The first biography by Celano gives a description of St. Francis that could hardly be surpassed for a description of nature mysticism.

Who would be able to express the very great love which he had for all things that were God's? Who would be able to tell of the sweetness he enjoyed when he contemplated in creatures the wisdom of the Creator, together with the Creator's power and goodness? Certainly he was frequently filled with a great and unspeakable joy from this sort of consideration when he looked upon the sun, while he beheld the moon, and while he gazed on the stars and the firmament. O simple piety, and pious simplicity. Even toward small worms he burned with a great love, for he had read this about the Savior: "I am a worm, and no man." Therefore he picked them up from the road and placed them in a safe spot so that they would not be crushed by the feet of those passing by. (*Legenda* 1.80)

Surely all of us have had similar experiences of creation, perhaps not as powerful, but real nonetheless: the experience of awe at the Grand Canyon, the Rocky Mountains, Niagara Falls, the redwood forests, sunrise and sunset.

But it is not only the grandeur and magnificence of so many creatures that evoke a sense of awe. It can also be the awareness of the small and apparently insignificant: the structure of the wing of a fly, the communal life of a colony of ants, and other things of this sort, which we normally pass by without even noticing. There are moments when we know that what we see is more than just so much chemistry.

What we need is a more concentrated sense awareness. With that, the beautiful objects of nature or of human culture can awaken us to levels of reality that we do not attend to in our everyday experience. This is not yet the mystical experience that Bonaventure sees as the goal of the journey, but it is a sense of meditative wonder that may serve to help us on the way. It is already a contact with God, but "through a glass, darkly."

We have mentioned two symbols employed by Bonaventure to express the meaning of creation. In *The Journey of the Soul into God* he uses other symbols. In this case, he describes creation as a ladder that the spiritual person can climb to arrive at ever deeper awareness of God, as did St. Francis. He uses also the symbol of the temple. In fact, this symbol, like that of the journey itself, or that of the ladder, reaches from these opening chapters to the climactic point at the end of the journey.

One needs to recall the structure of the temple in Jerusalem. One moves from the outer court to the interior, and then more deeply into its depths in the Holy of Holies, where is contained the Ark with the two angelic figures in the form of cherubim on its lid. Suffice it to say at this point that, for Bonaventure, we are still in the outer court of the temple. We can certainly feel the presence of St. Francis there. And, impressive as the court of the sensible world may be, this is not the end of the journey. Where we go from here will be the material of subsequent chapters.

A Word of Caution

With all this in mind, it may be difficult to understand the harsh language that Bonaventure uses to speak of the world in many of his other spiritual writings. Two observations might be in place concerning this issue.

First, Bonaventure is deeply grounded in Neoplatonic tradition both in his theology and in his spiritual doctrine. In fact, the main line of the Christian West, from the very earliest centuries of its history, has made extensive use of Neoplatonic elements. This probably is attributable to the fact that, while Neoplatonism is first of all a philosophical style, it seems to be more akin to religious and spiritual concerns than other possible philosophies. If nothing else, it leans strongly in the direction of a genuinely philosophical mysticism. Nevertheless, as a philosophical vision, it has an abiding distrust of material reality, including the human body.

By way of contrast, if we look at the biblical tradition concerning both creation and anthropology, we find a religious tradition that can describe the Creator who looks at the various creatures of the material world and calls them good. We might describe it as a religious tradition that saw genuine religious and spiritual significance in the material world, which has its ultimate origin in the creative love of God.

If we were to study the history of Christian Neoplatonism closely, we would discover that something of the tension between these two traditions tends to remain in the writings of most Christian Neoplatonists. We can think of St. Augustine as an early example. In the case of Bonaventure, we find a Platonically structured hierarchy of created beings. While all may be said to be good, some are "better" than others.

Most important for our reflections is the conviction that spiritual realities such as the human soul are higher on the hierarchy of being than the body together with all of material creation. Some of this hierarchial understanding we saw above in the distinction between vestige and image. What makes humanity an image lies, for Bonventure, principally in the area of the soul, with its faculties and its functions. Given this sense of hierarchy, it is quite possible for human persons to give an inappropriate importance to something that stands lower on the hierarchy rather than turning upward to things that are higher.

This leads to the second observation. While the spiritual writings of Bonaventure often use very strong, negative language about the world, if we look closer we will see that such texts do not refer to God's creation as such. In this spirituality, there is much room for enjoying the world of creation. Yet one who follows St. Francis or Bonaventure does not love the world of God's creation simply for its own sake, nor seek to find fulfillment for the yearnings of the human heart simply in the created world.

When all the exhortations about the world are finished, we do not really leave the world of God's creation. But we do try to resist a certain ethos of the human world of society and culture. This involves a way of relating to the world that is concerned excessively with sensual pleasures, or with such things as money, control, and power.

The harsh statements of Bonaventure refer not to God's creation as such but to distorted forms of human relations to the world of created things. These texts are concerned with the ways in which we give more weight to created goods than they can bear. To appreciate them as creatures of God that awaken us to a sense of the divine is one thing. To allow them to replace God in our spiritual journey is quite another thing. Created things are good and true, but theirs is a limited goodness and truth, had only by reason of participation in the divine goodness and truth. Reaching back to Augustine, Bonaventure explains this in terms of the image of an artist.

For things are true to the degree that they exist either in their own reality, or as universals, as they exist in the eternal Art and are expressed there. A thing is good, then, insofar as it is adequated to the intellect that causes it. But because it is not perfectly adequated to the reason that expresses or represents it, every creature is a lie, as Augustine says. (*SD* 3.8 [5:344]; reference to Augustine, *On True Religion* 61, 66, 83; and *83 Questions* q. 23)

This does not mean that creatures are bad. It means that they are a limited good and can be misread to our detriment if we attribute to them a greater truth than they possess. In the *Soliloquium*, Bonaventure writes:

Alas, O Lord, now I understand, but it shames me to admit all this: my eyes were deceived by the figure and beauty of creatures, and I failed to see that You are more beautiful than all creation to which You imparted but a drop of Your priceless splendor.... The sweetness of creatures deceived my taste, and I failed to notice that You are sweeter than honey, for it is You who imparted to honey and to every creature their sweetness, or rather Your own. For every good taste or flavor in the creatures is but a token of Your sweetness.... Thus, to one who sees properly, the charm of all creatures is but a sign that leads to Your eternal sweetness. (*Solil.* 1.3, n. 12–13 [8:33])

Or, again, we find a text that resonates strongly with the tragic experience of Willy Loman in Arthur Miller's play *Death of a Salesman*:

Reflect over and over on the following thought—not simply as something you have heard, but as something you have actually experienced: not only on the basis of words, but also on the basis of facts: how unstable is worldly wealth, how insecure is worldly success, and how futile is worldly fame. (*Solil.* 2.2 [8:44–45])

It seems clear that what we are dealing with here is not the world as God's creation but a world that has been worked over and shaped in terms of human values and projects. It is not a question of saying that the world of creation is somehow evil, but rather that the goodness of creation is a participated goodness and should not be allowed to take the place of the Absolute Goodness of God in our lives.

With the first text, we are led to ask about the symbolic meaning of all the goodness and beauty that we find in the world around us. We have just seen Bonaventure's delightful reflections on this dimension of human experience in the world.

In the second text we are invited to ask: What is it that can finally support us in our quest for a meaningful existence? Experience provides abundant evidence that all finite things, and especially all human constructs, can betray us in the end. It is not a question of saying that it is evil to be successful in one's career. But it is a question of saying you cannot ultimately trust such success. In both cases, in the Seraphic Doctor's view, what is problematic is the distorted importance we too easily give to what, by definition, are finite goods or humanly constructed projects.

[R]ecognize that your capacity is so great that no creature below God suffices to fill your desire. Hugh of St. Victor writes: "Every delight, sweetness, or beauty of a creature may touch the human heart, but none can fill it." And Anselm: "All abundance which is not God is poverty to me." And Gregory, in his *Ethics:* "The human soul is made to desire God. Anything below God that the soul desires is less than its true goal. It follows, then, that anything other than God will leave the soul unsatisfied." (*Solil.* 1.2, 6 [8:31])

From here we can see the logic of some form of asceticism or discipline. The issue is that we commonly fail to read the book of creation properly. We too easily give distorted importance to the finite things of the world which should be—in their goodness, truth, and beauty—symbols of the divine. Instead, we let them become ends in themselves, replacing the mystery of God, who alone can fill the emptiness that yawns in our depths. Discipline

and asceticism are indispensable in coming to terms with this
and eventually in finding the outer and inner quiet that is the
condition for a successful spiritual journey.

Ancient Greek philosophy formulated the maxim: Know
yourself! And Augustine once wrote: "I wish to know my God
and my soul. Nothing else? Nothing whatever" (Augustine,
Soliloquium 1.2.7). In a text reminiscent of both of these,
Bonaventure writes:

Therefore, O soul, make a daily examination of your life. Look
carefully to see how far you have advanced and how much further you have yet to go; look at the quality of your morals and
the character of your love; examine to what degree you are like
God and to what degree you are unlike God; take note of how
close to God, or how far removed from God you are. Remember
this always: it is better and more praiseworthy to know yourself than to ignore yourself while you come to know the course
of the stars, the power of herbs, the structure of human nature,
and the nature of animals—in short, all other things of heaven
and earth. Turn to your inner self, if not always, then at least
from time to time. Master your affections, guide your actions,
correct your ways. (*Solil.* 1.1, 2 [8:30])

Looking back at the way we have come, we can conclude that
this view, clearly rooted in the experience of St. Francis and
developed theologically by Bonaventure, might serve to awaken
us to a number of important concerns. It might alert us, first of
all, to the multiple dimensions of the world around us, and
awaken us to awe, admiration, and contemplative awareness of
those dimensions that do not appear as scientific data yet are real
factors in our experience.

It is a vision that calls us to recognize the beauty of things
independently of their practical usefulness. Surely questions
about use are inevitable. After all, we depend on other creatures
to support our own existence. But the contemplative, mystical
sense will have an impact on how we deal with such questions.

To accept the world as a gift does not mean that we do not use
it, nor do we look at it and tell the giver that it really is nothing.

Our first response to a gift is gratitude. In a similar way, our first response to the gift of our own existence is gratitude. It is in the awareness of creation that the Christian sense of the Eucharist is grounded.

In addition, at a very basic level, this vision might alert us to the intimate relation between ourselves and the physical world in which we live. We are so connected with the world and the world with us that the fate of one is inseparable from that of the other. In medieval terms, all the elements that go to make up the macrocosm are somehow present in the microcosm that is humanity. Hence, this is a spiritual vision that calls us to thoughtful respect for the world that has given us our physical life and sustains us in it.

It is interesting to reflect on the significance of this remarkable vision of cosmic reality in relation to the contemporary cosmological sense of the unitary character of the cosmos. From a scientific perspective, in terms of the best science available at the present time, all the elements that go to make up what we today call our cosmos appear to be deeply interrelated. Humanity, for its part, emerges out of the chemical web of the cosmos. In the famous line of Carl Sagan, we are stardust.

We are, in a sense, the cosmic process at a point where it has become aware of itself in the form of human consciousness and knowledge. We also have the freedom to take the cosmic process into our own hands and to shape it by humanly chosen values and ends. Thus, while we are deeply interwoven in the chemistry of the cosmos, there is a significant way in which we are distinctive. What we do with that distinctiveness can be of crucial significance in shaping our relations to the cosmic context of our life.

The vision of the world which we find in St. Francis and Bonaventure, then, is not simply a naïve religious dream. It offers the wisdom of a spiritual vision that may help us define our relation to the physical world as we know it today.

Open your eyes, alert your spiritual ears, unseal your lips, and apply your heart, so that in all creatures you may see, hear, praise, love, serve, glorify and honor God, lest the whole world rise up against you. For "the universe shall wage war against the foolish." On the contrary, it will be a matter of glory for the wise who can say with the prophet: "For you have given me, O Lord, a delight in your deeds, and I will rejoice in the work of your hands. How great are your works, O Lord! You have made all things in wisdom. The earth is filled with your creatures." (*JS* 1.15 [5:299])

Chapter 3

The World Inside

At this point, Bonaventure invites us to move from our reflections on the world outside to contemplate that mystery that lies hidden within ourselves, the human soul with its varied functions. As we make this move with Bonaventure, we might do well to recall a remarkable statement of the philosopher Alfred North Whitehead: "Religion is what the individual does with his own solitariness." He then goes on to write: ". . . religion is solitariness; and if you are never solitary, you are never religious" (*Religion in the Making* [New York: World Publishing Co., 1960], 16).

One could certainly argue about how adequate this is as a description of religion, but one thing is clear. It certainly points to a crucial dimension of religion without which religious systems run the danger of becoming pure external formalities. At its depth, writes Whitehead, "the religious insight is the grasp of this truth: That the order of the world, the depth of reality of the world, the value of the world in its whole and in its parts, the beauty of the world, the zest of life, the peace of life, and the mastery of evil, are all bound together" (*Religion in the Making*, 115).

Surely this statement reveals a deep insight into human experience and the meaning of religion in relation to that experience. If we look at it from a theological perspective, we might describe it this way. In the most basic sense, we are "from God and for God." After all has been said about our origin from our parents, our grandparents, and the rest of our family history, finally we are "from" God. On the other hand, when we have said all that is to be said about future plans, career, and projects, ultimately we are "for" God.

This describes from a theological perspective what we experience psychologically. There is a point at the inner core of our experience that can never be touched by any other human being. No one can see through your eyes. No matter how fine one's community experience may be in family life or elsewhere, who you are deep inside is really your own most personal secret. You may be able to talk about it to others, but finally no other human person can really know you as you know yourself and as you desire to be known. If you can be touched at this level at all, it will be by God. Bonaventure cites Augustine in a significant way:

Listen to what Augustine, the great lover of God, has to say in his *Confessions:* "When I love God, it is not bodily beauty that I love, nor temporal glory, nor the brilliance of a light that appeals to the eyes, nor sweet melodies, nor sweet-smelling ointments, nor manna, nor honey, nor limbs made for bodily embrace: it is none of these things that I love when I love God. But what do I love? I love a kind of light, a kind of voice, a certain fragrance, a certain food, a certain embrace of my inner self. Within my soul there shines a light that space cannot contain; there is a sound that time cannot still; there is a fragrance that no wind can blow away; there is a savoring that is not diminished by eating; there is something that clings so tightly to my soul that satiety does not tear us apart." (*Solil.* 1.4, 44 [8:43])

What we do with our solitariness! At some point this is a crucial issue of religion. When everything is said about the relations that make up our lives, and all is said about religious teachings, laws, rituals, and celebrations, religion is what we do with our solitariness. It is what we do with that most intimate, personal fact that, even in the midst of swarming human activity, we are and remain alone inside. What do we do with this fact? What do we think about it? How do we deal with it?

In our culture, there is a strong tendency to block this out; to drown it out with noise and activity. We are forever assaulted with the portable radios and headsets carried everywhere on the street, on the running path, in buses, and in trains, in the early morning hours and throughout the day, well into the night. And there is the pervasive presence of the portable telephone even on remote ski slopes in the Rocky Mountains of Colorado and the Sierra Nevadas of California so that one may always be reached and always be in contact.

This is not only a marketing phenomenon; it is also a religious phenomenon. We cannot bear to turn off all the external signals that come at us through these remarkable technological devices. Why is that? Is it, perhaps, because of fear of the solitariness we will experience within? And yet, despite all our efforts to silence the voice of that inner silence, it does not go away. And the need for personal depth remains. What does one do with one's solitariness? This raises the issue of the contemplative dimension in human life.

The contemplative dimension in the life of St. Francis appears in all the early biographies. They speak of Francis's periods of withdrawal to remote places and caves to pray, and we know about the Rule for Hermitages as part of the early history of the order. Bonaventure describes Francis in the following way:

In prayer he had learned that the presence of the Holy Spirit which he longed for was granted more intimately to those who pray to the degree that the Holy Spirit found them withdrawn from the rush of worldly affairs. Therefore seeking out lonely places, he used to go to deserted areas and abandoned churches to spend the night in prayer. There he often endured horrible fights with demons who struggled with him physically and tried to pull him away from his desire for prayer. But armed with heavenly weapons, the more vehemently he was attacked by the enemy, the stronger he became in practicing virtue and the more fervent in prayer. (*LM* 10.3 [8:533])

This contemplative dimension of Francis was so strong in the estimation of Bonaventure that it could be seen as the final meaning of his way of life.

Above all, the Alverna experience as Bonaventure describes it in *The Life of St. Francis* and in his sermons highlights this dimension. The experience on Alverna is seen preeminently as a contemplative-mystical experience. And it is the epitome and summary of St. Francis's life.

The world of God's creation does indeed have an outside. But it has an inside as well. And its inside is where human beings encounter their solitariness and the possible depth of their relation with God. For a medieval theologian such as Bonaventure, the inside of the world is the question of the human soul and its remarkable functions.

The Soul as Image of God

The early Franciscan theologians developed the contemplative dimension not only in terms of St. Francis's nature mysticism but also, especially in the case of Bonaventure, by making use of the Augustinian tradition of the inner way. As we have seen in the preceding chapter, there is no doubt that, in the mind of Bonaventure, the experience of the world of nature can trigger a deep experience of wonder, meditation, and prayer. But beyond this, Bonaventure urges us, after we have learned to see the world in this way, to turn to the world of our inner experience. And there we will find even more remarkable things.

With this in mind, we recall the spiritual journey of Augustine. At one point in his *Confessions,* he describes how he has looked everywhere to find whatever it is that he was looking for. He had tried a variety of philosophies and youthful excesses, but he had found nothing to satisfy his restless heart. He addressed God in the following way:

> Being thus admonished to return to myself, under your leadership I entered into my inmost being. This I could do, for you became my helper. I entered there, and by my soul's eye, such as it was, I saw above that same eye of my soul, above my mind, an unchangeable light. (*Confessions* 7.10)

More elaborate, but along a similar line, Augustine writes in his slim tract *On True Religion:*

> Do not go abroad. Return within yourself. For truth dwells in the inner person. If you find that your nature is subject to change, then

transcend yourself. But remember when you do this that you must transcend yourself even as a rational soul. Move toward that place where the light of reason is kindled. What is it that every good reasoning person attains but truth? And yet truth is not attained by reasoning, but is itself the goal of all who reason. There is an agreeableness than which none can be greater. Come to agree with it. Confess that you are not as it is. It has to do no seeking, but you reach it by seeking, not in space, but by a disposition of mind, so that the inner person may come to agree with the indwelling truth in a pleasure that is not low and carnal but supremely spiritual. (*On True Religion* 39.72)

Here Augustine describes in impressive terms the "turn inward." Not having found what he was seeking in the world outside himself, he now turns to the world within, to that remarkable cosmos that resides within the world of the human soul. And where is one more solitary than in the depths of one's inner world? Throughout the *Confessions* and in other works such as *On the Trinity* and *The Teacher*, Augustine will show himself to be an outstanding master of the spirituality of the "inner way."

Following the lead of this master, Bonaventure, having completed the first two levels of his analysis of the spiritual journey by the examination of the world of sensible things and of the human sense experience of these things, now invites us to move in another direction. Instead of continuing to look outward, let us now look inward, into the world of our own interiority.

The first two stages, by leading us to God by means of the vestiges through which God shines forth in all creatures, have brought us to the point of entering into ourselves, that is, into our mind, where the divine image shines forth. It is here that . . . we re-enter into our very selves; and as it were, leaving the outer court, we should strive to see God through a mirror in the holy place, that is, in the space in front of the tabernacle. Here, as from a candelabrum, the light of truth glows upon the face of our mind, in which the image of the most blessed Trinity shines in splendor. (*JS* 3.1 [5:303])

In the *Journey of the Soul into God* this step leads Bonaventure to reflect on the way in which the human being is more than a distant vestige of God, but is truly an image of the Trinity. He develops this by reflecting on the mystery of the soul's powers, faculties, and functions. As we have seen with the reflections on the world outside ourselves, Bonaventure approaches the issue at two levels; so also here, in viewing the world inside ourselves, his discussion takes place on two levels. The first involves reflections on the nature of the soul precisely as an image of God. The second looks at the operation of divine grace within the soul, cleansing it from sin and bringing it to perfection.

To develop his viewpoint, Bonaventure reaches back to elements of the Augustinian anthropology which the African Doctor had developed in his work *On the Trinity.* Augustine, it will be recalled, felt dissatisifed with the sort of physical metaphors often used in the early fathers to discuss the mystery of the Trinity. He felt that they were too crude and may well be more harmful than helpful. In his attempt to move beyond these physical metaphors, he developed what has come to be known as the psychological model of trinitarian theology. This style was to have a massive influence on Western trinitarian theology down to the present time.

This may be seen as another example of Augustine's tendency to move into the world of human consciousness. If God is thought of as supreme Spirit, then we might find some helpful insights into the mystery of the divine by probing into the world of created spirit. For Augustine, if the human person is to be understood as an image of God, then the analysis of human reality might provide better analogies than the older physical analogies.

It is by looking inward into ourselves where we see something of the dynamism of spirit-in-act that we may find clues to what is meant by the purest Spirit-in-act. Augustine's attempt to find helpful metaphors leads him to two significant triadic structures. The first is mind–knowledge–love, and the second is memory–intelligence–will. While Bonaventure does not use these extensively in his trinitarian theology, he does employ this tradition for laying out his anthropology. He will use especially the triad of memory–intelligence–will.

Bonaventure will also follow Augustine in an unusual understanding of what is meant by *memory*. The common understanding of the term has to do with the way in which the human person retains something of experiences from the past. We can remember things that we did, or things that happened to us years ago. Even though these things may not be at the foreground of our consciousness for long periods of time, they remain deep inside us and can be called forth by a variety of means. But for Bonaventure, the term *memory* has a broader meaning. It involves not only the past but the present and the future also; and in this way it reflects something of the mystery of God's eternity.

In the soul, which is the image of God, there is the memory of past things, the understanding of present things, and the anticipation of future things. These things, which succeed each other in diverse moments of time, are gathered and bound together simultaneously in the soul which is a spiritual substance. And yet, because the soul is limited and receives things into itself from outside, it does not enjoy total simultaneity. God, on the other hand, receives nothing and is limited in no way. Therefore God is to be understood necessarily as having all things simultaneously present, without beginning or end. And this is how we are to understand eternity. (*Trin.* 5.1, resp. [5:90])

Augustine had thought of memory in similar ways. But he was fascinated further by the fact that there seem to be other things going on inside us that we cannot fully account for in terms of our ordinary understanding of human knowledge, and Bonaventure would follow him in this regard. The description of memory that we have just seen does not exhaust the possible meaning of the term, nor does it explain the source of certain kinds of knowledge.

We seem to know certain things that we apparently have never learned. How do we account for this? In the background of this style of reflection is the ancient Socratic and Platonic tradition of memory which still plays a role in so-called Socratic approaches to teaching. Does the teacher simply feed the student with data and information, or does the teacher, at certain levels, help awaken the student's memory?

Augustine is led to envision memory not simply as the place where we hold our past experiences but as a much deeper well of preconscious connection with the self (memory of the self), and finally with God (memory of God). Out of this preconscious well flows eventually a consciousness of self that can be named, analyzed, and thought about. Bonaventure will use the term "memory" in a similar way. It is impossible to come to a conscious self-knowledge without that preconscious presence to self involved in memory, he argues. The text of the *Journey of the Soul into God* is a clear example of this.

In a technical discussion of three levels at which we can speak of the activity of memory, Bonaventure has described how memory is the power to retain temporal things. It can also hold the forms abstracted from sense experience. But, at a third level, he speaks of the way eternal principles of logic and of the sciences seem to be with us in an almost innate manner. For example, if we know the meaning of the words *whole* and *part,* the truth of the proposition that says "The whole is greater than the part" is self-evident.

This sort of knowledge, which seems to be innate, suggests that the soul is somehow in contact with what Platonic philosophy would call the world of Ideas. Christian theology, at least from the time of Augustine, had situated these Ideas in the mind of God.

From the third level, we conclude that memory has an undying light present to itself in which it recalls unchanging truths. And thus, from the operations of memory, it is clear that the soul itself is an image of God and a similitude so present to itself and having God so present that it actually grasps God and potentially "is capable of possessing God and of becoming a partaker in God." (*JS* 3.2 [5:303])

All of this comes to bear very clearly when we look at Bonaventure's more detailed statement about the relation of memory to the other functions of the soul:

Enter into yourself, therefore, and see that your mind loves itself most fervently. But it could not love itself if it did not know itself; and it could not know itself if it were not present to itself in memory, for whatever we grasp with our understanding must first be present to us in our memory. From this you can see, not with the eye of the body but with the eye of the mind, that your soul has three powers. If you consider the activites of these three powers and their relationships, you will be able to see God through yourself as through an image. And this, indeed, is to see "through a mirror in an obscure manner." (*JS* 3.1 [5:303])

Bonaventure's analysis of intelligence or understanding is, in a sense, an anticipation of an argument that will appear more fully when we contemplate the names of God. In the present level of reflection, Bonaventure focuses on the importance of knowing the meaning of the terms that will be used in formulating judgments and developing arguments. But the process of defining terms leads us from concrete particulars to wider and more general perspectives, and finally to universal terms. Only when we reach the universal do we arrive at that on which all the previous stages are grounded, and only then do we know the object of our concern in the truest sense of the word. Bonaventure concludes that unless we know Being *per se*, we will not fully know the definition of any particular being. Put in a different way, the human mind cannot come to an assured knowledge of what created beings are without some knowledge of that pure, simple, eternal Being in which all things are grounded.

Our intellect cannot come to a full knowledge of any created things unless it is aided by the knowledge of that Being that is most pure, most actual, most complete and absolute; that which is Being simply and eternally, in which the principles of all other things are found in their pure form. Or, how could the intellect know that a particular being is incomplete and defective if it had no knowledge of a Being free of all defect? (*JS* 3.3 [5:304])

As this line of thought is drawn out to include both the making of judgments and the development of arguments or syllogisms, it eventually leads to the claim that, in fact, we do have certain knowledge; and that this fact cannot be explained in terms of the objects we know, or in terms of our intellect itself.

Since things have an existence in the human mind, in their own reality, and in the eternal art, the truth which they have either in the human mind or in themselves is not sufficient for certitude, since both of these are subject to change—unless in some way the soul comes to these things as they are in the eternal art. (*KC* q. 4, resp. [5:23])

Thus, Bonaventure moves from the fact that there is some certitude in human knowledge to the explanation of this fact through some form of divine illumination.

[This certitude] comes from the exemplarity in the eternal art. It is in relation to this that things have an aptitude and a relation to each other according to the representation which they have in the eternal art. As Augustine says in *On True Religion,* "The light of one who reasons truly is enkindled by that truth, and strives to return to that truth." From this it is manifestly clear that our intellect is joined to the eternal Truth itself, and that our intellect could not know anything with certitude unless it were being instructed by that light. (*JS* 3.3 [5:304])

And then there is the faculty of the will by which we can deliberate, judge, and make choices. The argument here is similar to that about the intellect. The principal difference is that the object of the will is the good. One cannot deliberate about, make judgments, and make choices about lesser degrees of the good unless, in some way, one has an awareness of the supreme Good. For the will to function effectively, therefore, some notion of the supreme Good must be imprinted on the soul.

[D]esire is directed principally to that which moves one the most. That which most moves one's desire is that which one loves the most. That which one loves the most is to be happy. But there is no happiness except through the possession of the best and final end. Human desire, therefore, seeks nothing other than the highest Good, or something that leads to that Good, or something that resembles that Good. So great is the power of the highest Good that nothing can be loved by the creature except by reason of a desire for the highest Good. And anyone who takes the image or the copy in place of the truth is in error and goes astray. (*JS* 3.4 [5:304])

As had been the case in Augustine, so here in Bonaventure it is through the analysis of these three faculties—memory, intellect, and will—and their functions and interrelations that one is led to a sense of the triadic, relational nature of spirit-being in the human person, and one is led also to the sense of how the soul— the image of God—is related to God in terms of the divine eternity (in memory), the divine truth (in intelligence), and the divine goodness (in will). Recognizing the limitations which must be placed on all human attempts to speak about God, Bonaventure concludes:

These three—the generating mind, the word, and love—are present in the soul as memory, intelligence, and will; they are consubstantial, co-equal and contemporary, and mutually immanent. Therefore, if God is a perfect spirit, then God has memory, intelligence, and will; God has both a Word begotten and a Love breathed forth. These are necessarily distinct, since one is produced by the other. They are distinguished neither essentially nor accidentally, but personally. When the soul reflects on itself, it rises through itself as through a mirror to speculation about the Blessed Trinity of Father, Word, and Love; three Persons co-eternal, co-equal, and consubstantial, so that whatever is in any one is in the others, but one is not the other, but all three are one God. (*JS* 3.5 [5:305])

From all of this we can begin to see how, in the thought of Bonaventure, it is possible for us to come to some sense of the mystery of God by reflecting on the mystery of the human soul, and particularly on the faculties of memory, intelligence, and will. Since, in fact, we are reflecting on the mystery of spiritual being in ourselves, this can be seen as a fuller reflection of God than what we discovered in the first two steps of this journey. For here we are reflecting on the image of God.

We have spoken earlier about the Neoplatonic tendency to envision an organically structured hierarchy of being, moving from the most sublime to the most opaque—that is, from the most exalted forms of spiritual being to the humblest forms of material being. In Bonaventure's analysis, we have seen the language of vestige and image as reflections of that tendency. In his spiritual teaching and in his theology of grace, this reflects a lesser and a higher degree of similarity to the divine. But the deepest meaning of the image will take us further into the meaning of the soul.

In Bonaventure's understanding, to speak of the soul as an image of God is to describe the human being as an openness, or as a potential to a yet deeper communication of the divine than we have just seen in the previous section on the faculties of the soul. It is this potential that has been fulfilled in the most profound way in the incarnation of the Word in Jesus of Nazareth. But the same potency for a depth of divine self-communication which made the incarnation possible without destroying the humanity of Jesus lies in the depths of each human being. In the case of Jesus, this potency is brought to act by a union with one who is Son of God by nature. In all others, it is brought to act by the mystery of adoptive filiation. In an extraordinary Christmas sermon, Bonaventure says:

The ability of human nature to be united in a unity of person with the divine—which is the most noble of all the receptive potencies implanted in human nature—is reduced to act so that it would not be a mere empty potency. And insofar as it is reduced to act, the perfection of the entire created order is realized, for in that one being the unity of all reality is brought to consummation. (*Sermon II on the Nativity of the Lord* [9:110])

The christological implications of this text are exceptional. For our purposes here, it is sufficient to point out that, as here described, the deepest potential of the entire created order is found in human nature, which we have just described as an image of the divine. To be an image, therefore, means to be open to a deeper communication of the divine than that which is given in the fact of creation. And when that deeper divine self-communication is effective in the human person, that person reflects an even more intense similarity to God; the image becomes a similitude or a likeness. God has created humanity and equipped it in such a way that it is destined for the most profound union with God:

From this we may conclude that the created world is like a book in which the trinity that creates it is reflected, represented, and described at three levels of expression: as a vestige, as an image, and as a similitude. The reality of the vestige is found in every creature; the reality of the image is found only in intellectual creatures or rational spirits; the reality of the similitude is found only in those who are conformed to God. Through these levels, as it were on the rungs of a ladder, the human mind is designed in its nature to ascend gradually to the supreme Principle who is God. (*Brevil.* 2.12 [5:230])

In another text, Bonaventure makes use of cosmic imagery and looks back to the biblical fourth day of creation, where God is described as creating the celestial lights. He uses these resources to speak in symbolic terms of the nature of the contemplative soul.

This idea that our understanding might be suspended through contemplation can be understood in terms of the work of the fourth day on which the lights were made. For only that soul which has the sun and the moon and the stars in its firmament is suspended in contemplation. Consider what the world would have been like, if there had been no sun, moon, or stars in the firmament. It would have been nothing but a kind of dark mass, for even the night with only the light of the stars is dark and frightening. So it is with the soul. A soul that does not have the grace of contemplation is like a firmament without lights. But a soul that does have that grace is like a firmament adorned with lights. And as a heaven that does not have these lights is different from another heaven that has them, so a soul that does not have (this grace) differs from another that has it. The difference is like that between an angel and a beast. For a person who lacks these lights is like a beast, with his face turned down toward the earth like an animal. But the person full of lights is fully angelic. (*SD* 20.2 [5:425])

See, therefore, how close the soul is to God. See how memory in its operation brings us to eternity; intelligence brings us to truth; and our power of choice brings us to the highest good. (*JS* 3.4 [5:305])

All of this gives a very positive emphasis to the beauty and dignity of the human soul. And yet Bonaventure is fully aware of weaknesses in the soul. Despite the soul's remarkable potential for the divine, it is clear that "few perceive the First Principle within themselves." This Bonaventure explains in the following terms:

Because the human mind is distracted by cares, it does not enter into itself through memory; because it is obscured with sense images, it does not come back to itself through intelligence; and because it is drawn by concupiscence, it does not return to itself through the desire for interior sweetness and spiritual joy. Because it is totally immersed in things of sense, the soul cannot re-enter into itself as the image of God. (*JS* 4.1 [5:306])

These statements must be seen in relation to what is said in the *Soliloquy*. There Bonaventure clearly distinguishes the soul as formed by God in creation and as deformed by sin through human failure, and therefore in need of being reformed by the grace of God in Christ. Concerning the first, he says:

It seems to me that the beauty of your nature consists in this: that the image of the most blessed Trinity is impressed in you naturally for your adornment.... Behold, my soul, what a wonderful and inestimable dignity it is to be not only a vestige of the Creator, as all creatures are, but to be also His image, which is the privilege of rational creatures. (*Solil.* 1.2, 3 [8:30])

But that glorious nature in which the soul was formed has been miserably deformed by human sinfulness:

Now that you realize how generously you have been formed by nature, consider how viciously you have been deformed by sin. "Remember the enormity of your sin, miserable and wretched soul. Let your shouting and your lamentation reach up to heaven." . . . Remember, my soul, for what price it was that you sold your beauty, for what advantage that you threw away your honor, for what purpose that you so disfigured your face. Such great goods you exchanged for such a vile reward. (*Solil.* 1.3, 10 [8:33])

The Image Reformed by Grace

All this is indicative of the fact that, noble as the soul may be in terms of its created nature, it is, in fact, in a fallen condition. The soul, formed in such noble terms by God, has been deformed throughout human history and must be re-formed. If it truly desires to enter on the spiritual journey, it must be purged and lifted up by the divine light. This is the work of God's grace in the human person. And with grace come the theological virtues "by which the soul is purified, enlightened, and perfected" (*JS* 4.3 [5:306]). This is done through the mediation of Christ.

When one has fallen, it is necessary to lie there unless there is someone at hand to help lift up the fallen person. In a similar way, our soul could not be lifted up out of these things of sense completely so as to see itself and the eternal Truth in itself if that Truth had not assumed a human form in Christ, thus becoming a ladder to restore the first ladder that had been broken in Adam. (*JS* 4.2 [5:306])

Using the language of Dionysian hierarchical thought, Bonaventure here describes Christ as the "supreme Hierarch, who purifies, enlightens, and perfects His spouse, that is, the entire church and every sanctified soul" (*JS* 4.5 [5:307]). It is important to note here that the life of grace and the spiritual life are described not as something that draws the individual away from the community of the church, but draws each into more perfect harmony.

The image of our mind, therefore, is to be clothed over with the three theological virtues by which the soul is purified, enlightened, and perfected. In this way the image is reformed and made to be like the heavenly Jerusalem and a part of the church militant, which is the offspring of the heavenly Jerusalem, according to the Apostle. (*JS* 4.3 [5:306])

The text then goes on to make explicit the role of Christ in the process of reforming the soul:

Therefore, the soul believes in, hopes in, and loves Jesus Christ, Who is the Word incarnate, uncreated, and inspired, that is, the way and the truth and the life. When by faith it believes in Christ as the uncreated Word and the splendor of the Father, it recovers its spiritual hearing and vision; its hearing in order to receive the teachings of Christ; and its vision to look upon the splendor of His light. When, however, with hope it yearns to receive the inspired Word through desire and affection, it recovers its spiritual sense of smell. When it embraces the incarnate Word in charity, receiving delight from Him and passing into Him through ecstatic love, it recovers its sense of taste and touch. When these spiritual senses have been restored so that the soul sees, hears, smells, tastes, and embraces its Spouse, it can sing like the bride of the *Canticle of Canticles,* which was written for the sake of the exercise of contemplation at this fourth stage, which "no one knows except one who receives it." This occurs in affective experience more than in rational thought. On this level, when the inner senses are restored to see the highest beauty, to hear the highest harmony, to smell the highest fragrance, to taste the highest delicacy, and to apprehend that which is most delightful, the soul is disposed to mental elevation through devotion, admiration, and exultation, in accordance with the three exclamations which are in the *Canticle of Canticles.* (*JS* 4.3 [5:306])

Here as in many other places, Bonaventure uses the language of the threefold way to describe three dimensions of the spiritual journey. This language can be traced back to Dionysius.

It is necessary, therefore, to ascend by three steps in accordance with the threefold way; namely the purgative way, which consists in being cleansed from sin; the illuminative way, which consists in the imitation of Christ; and the unitive way, which consists in union with the Spouse. (*TW* 3.1 [8:12])

The journey, therefore, involves what Bonaventure calls three hierarchic acts: purgation, which involves removing all obstacles that stand in the way; illumination, which means learning to see with the eye of Christ; and consummation, which involves experiencing ever deeper union with God in love. These three might best be seen not as a chronological flowchart that defines so much time to be spent in purgation, and so much time in illumination, and so on. Rather, the hierarchic acts represent dimensions of spirituality at all times as long as we are in history. One always needs purgation and further illumination to enter more fully into union with God.

The issue of purgation will raise the question of asceticism. Illumination raises the need to develop a truly spiritual vision of reality and not to remain at the level of empirical observation and evaluation. And the goal is always deeper love. The soul needs to be:

Lifted up to the heights, above everything sensible, imaginable, and intelligible . . . because God is beyond demonstration, definition, opinion, estimation, or investigation. Consequently, God is beyond our understanding and yet is totally desirable. (*TW* 1.17 [8:7])

The life of grace and the virtues, in Bonaventure's understanding, is a process of radical transformation as the human person is drawn ever more deeply into the trinitarian life of God.

One who wishes to ascend to God must first of all avoid sin which deforms nature. It is necessary, then, to bring those natural powers under grace which reforms them. And this is done

through prayer; prayer for that justice which purifies in the conduct of our life; and prayer for that knowledge which illumines
in the form of meditation; and prayer for that wisdom which
leads to perfection in contemplation. . . . And since grace is the
foundation of the rightness of the will and the clear illumination of reason, we must pray first of all; then we must live in
a holy manner, and thirdly, we must look upon the reflections
of truth, and by gazing on them, we must rise gradually until
we arrive at the high mountain "where the God of gods is seen
in Sion." (*JS* 1.8 [5:298])

More eloquent testimony to the importance of grace as the foundation of the spiritual journey is found in the following:

Grace, indeed, is a gift that is bestowed and infused immediately by God. For, with it and in it we receive the Holy Spirit,
who is the uncreated gift, that best and most perfect gift that
comes down from the God of Lights through the incarnate
Word. . . . It is this gift that purges, illumines, and perfects the
soul; that vivifies it, reforms it, and strengthens it; that elevates
it, assimilates it to God, and unites it with God, and thus
makes the soul acceptable to God. (*Brevil.* 5.1 [5:252])

Grace itself can be described by Bonaventure with the term
deiformitas, God-likeness. This does not mean that the human
being becomes metaphysically divine. But it does mean that
through the spiritual journey the human person is opened ever
more to the divine self-communication that enters into the depths
of the person and begins the process of radical re-formation (or
transformation) through which it moves higher on the scale of the
hierarchy of God-likeness.

Finally, since God, in the final analysis, is a triune God, the
similitude in the graced human person involves a depth of relation to the persons of the Trinity. As we have seen above, all proceeds from the Father, through the Son, in the Spirit. The work of
the Spirit in the human person is, essentially, to draw that person
more deeply into the mystery of the Son and thus into the Son's
relation to both the Father and the Spirit.

In this sense, Bonaventure can describe the relationship of

grace as *filiation*. This means, specifically, that the life of grace, which transforms the person within, flows outward to the living of the virtues that lie at the center of the life of the incarnate Word; for these values give concrete expression to the mystery of the one who stands at the center of the Trinity and at the center of all created reality.

To grow in the spiritual journey is to allow one's personal life to become centered on that reality and to become more deeply like the Son who is that center. The deepest meaning of that centering is to come to that humble self-awareness in which one recognizes how radically one comes from God and how deeply one is oriented to God as to the final end of the human journey. To recognize this, and to see to what degree this reality has been distorted by our fallen history is to be poor in spirit. It is the condition for any significant growth in the life of grace. To grow in grace, then, is to grow in God-likeness by becoming more like Christ. To grow in Christ-likeness is to enter more deeply into the Word's relation to the Father and the Spirit:

If, then, the rational soul is to become worthy of eternal happiness, it must participate in a God-conforming influence. Such an influence, since it comes from God, conforms to God, and leads to God as to our end, restores the image in our spirit, conforming it to the most blessed Trinity and affecting it not only as part of the order of creation, but also in terms of the righteousness of the will and the repose of beatitude. And since a soul so favored is brought back immediately to God and conformed immediately to God, therefore this grace is granted immediately by God acting as the Source of grace. Therefore, as the image of God comes forth immediately from God so also does the similitude, which is the same image but now in its God-conformed perfection. It is called, therefore, the image of the new creation. (*Brevil.* 5.1 [5:252–53])

Following a similar line of thought, Bonaventure writes at the conclusion of his *Disputed Questions on the Mystery of the Trinity:*

... eternal life consists in this alone, that the rational spirit, which comes forth from the most blessed Trinity and is a like-

ness of the Trinity, should return like a certain intelligible circle—through memory, intelligence, and will—to the most blessed
Trinity by God-conforming glory. (*Trin.* q. 8, 7 [5:115])

The Mystical Vine expresses the whole of this vision of the soul—
formed, deformed, and reformed—in the following words:

The One who is so good and so great desires your embraces
and is waiting to embrace you. He inclines toward you the
flower of His head, pierced with many thorns, and invites you
to receive the kiss of peace, as if to say: See how I was disfigured, transfixed, and beaten in order that I could place you
upon My shoulder—My sheep who goes astray—and bring you
back to the paradise of heavenly pastures. Now you, for your
part: be moved with pity for My wounds; and just as you now
see Me, "place Me as a seal upon your heart, and as a seal
upon your arm"; so that in every thought of your heart, in every
work of your hands, you may be found to resemble Me who
am wearing these seals. When I created you, I conformed you
to the likeness of My divinity. In order to re-form you, I became
conformed to the likeness of your humanity. Do you, who did
not keep the form of My divinity which was impressed on you
when you were created, keep at least that imprint of your
humanity which was stamped on me when you were re-formed.
If you did not stay as I created you, at least stay as I have re-
created you. If you do not understand how great were the powers I granted you in creating you, understand at least how great
were the miseries I accepted for you in your humanity, in re-
creating you, and in re-forming you for joys much greater than
those for which I had originally formed you. I became a visible
human being so that you might see Me and so love Me, since,
as long as I was unseen and invisible in My divinity, I was not
loved properly. As a price for My incarnation and passion, give
Me yourself, you for whom I became flesh and for whom I suf-
fered. I have given Myself to you; now give yourself to Me. (*MV*
24.3 [8:188])

In his early *Commentary on the Sentences* (*II Sent.* prooe. [2:3ff.])
Bonaventure comments on the text of Ecclesiastes 7:30: "God

created humanity upright," that is, standing straight and erect. He interprets this text in such a way as to indicate how the term *image* can be seen to designate a task or a goal to be undertaken in human life. He explains this in relation to three activities of human experience: intelligence, will, and ability to control. It is in terms of these three abilities that the human person is called to stand upright, reflecting God as an image of the divine in the created world.

Our intellect is made to be upright when it comes to know things for what they really are, limited expressions of the very truth of God. Our will is made to be upright when it embraces the good in things precisely as a limited share in the goodness of God. And our ability to control is made to be upright when the quality of human creativity conforms to and expresses the loving quality of God's creative action.

Human beings, therefore, as God would have us, are created to function as images of God, standing upright in the world, a living revelation of the truth, goodness, and loving power of God in the world. To the degree that we turn ourselves to God in this way, to that degree the finite things in the world will fall into place. With our minds in harmony with divine truth, our wills in harmony with divine goodness, and our ability to engage our creative energies in harmony with God's creative love, we are called to participate in the creative process by which the world will be brought to its God-intended goal.

By discovering the truth of the world as a participation in God's truth, by loving the goodness of the world as a participation in God's goodness, and by continuing God's creative love in human society and history—it is in this way that we live out what it means to be created in God's image. It is in this way that the soul becomes hierarchized, or brought back into harmony within itself and in relation to the world of God's creation.

Thus, in reflecting on the soul as an image of God, Bonaventure has led us to ponder deeply the mystery of our own interior world, to see its potential and its obviously limited condition, and to see it remarkably restored by the grace of God to become a similitude of the divine. The most profound union with God is preeminently the gift of grace. It is this union with the divine that arises to some level of awareness in the mystical experience as Bonaventure sees it.

Bonaventure concludes his reflections on the soul reformed by grace in the following way.

When our mind is filled with all these intellectual lights, it is, as it were, a house of God inhabited by the divine Wisdom. It becomes a daughter, a spouse, and a friend of God; it becomes a member of Christ, the Head, a sister and co-heir. It becomes also a temple of the Holy Spirit, grounded in faith, elevated through hope, and dedicated to God through holiness of mind and body. It is the most sincere love of Christ that brings all this about, a love that is poured into our hearts by the Holy Spirit who has been given to us. Without this Spirit, we cannot come to know the divine mysteries. For no one can know the things of a human person except the spirit of that person that abides within. Thus, the mysteries of God are known by no one but the Spirit of God. Let us, therefore, be rooted and grounded in love, that we may comprehend with all the Saints, what is the length of eternity, what is the breadth of liberality, what is the height of majesty, and what is the depth of that discerning wisdom. (*JS* 4.8 [5:308])

Chapter 4

The World Above

We might use the term *metaphysical mysticism* to designate a level of reflection that, to most of us, might seem to be purely philosophical. We may be inclined at first to see this mode of reflection to be really no different from that of the great Neoplatonist philosophical mystic Plotinus. He seems to have made a remarkable ascent up the ladder of being while focusing his mind on the true, the good, and the One. His experience seems to be a form of purely philosophical mysticism. It would have a significant impact on Christian tradition, but it was consistently seen as philosophy and not as theology.

Bonaventure, who is well aware of this tradition, has explicitly set up his task in a different way. As we have seen, Bonaventure assumes a person of faith as the subject of the journey he is describing. This, together with what we have seen concerning the role of divine grace, makes it clear that, at least in Bonaventure's mind, what follows here is not a purely philosophical adventure.

Together with this, if we recall how, in the history of Christian thought and spirituality, the tradition of philosophical thought was commonly used to form theological terminology and to develop theological thought, it will become easier to understand the theological overtones of what Bonaventure invites us into at this point.

God as the Mystery of Being

We have looked at the world of sense objects outside our consciousness. We have looked at the world within ourselves. We are now invited to look at that reality that is above ourselves. In terms of the symbol of the temple, we have already moved from the outer court to the inner court. At this point, we move deeper into the temple into the Holy of Holies, where the ark of the covenant is kept. There we see the ark surmounted by two cherubim facing each other over the mercy seat.

To understand better what Bonaventure is about at this point, we need to recall in a special way what happened to the text of Exodus 3:14 when it was translated from Hebrew into Greek. Moses has been told by God to return to Egypt to lead the people out. Moses responds to God by asking how he should identify God when the people ask who has sent him.

It is at this point that the Hebrew text provides a way of speaking about God that some scholars see as a puzzle or as a simple refusal to give a name. Others suggest that it might be seen in the context of covenant theology as a promise of saving presence. Few if any biblical scholars today are willing to see the Hebrew formulation as equivalent to the Greek text together with all its apparent philosophical overtones. Yet that is the way in which it was read by Christians for centuries, including the time of Bonaventure.

What stands out in that reading of the Greek translation of the text is the fact that the name which God gives to Moses is identical with the Greek word used by the philosophers of antiquity to name the object of their concern: Being. What we are confronted with in Greek is almost impossible to translate except through some form of paraphrase. Since, in terms of grammar, it is the present participle form of the Greek word for "to be" preceded by a definite article, a very literal but awkward translation might be "the being-one." Attempts to offer a more congenial-sounding translation suggest the following. God says to Moses: "I am who I am." Or God replies to the question of Moses by saying that Moses should tell the people that "I AM sent me."

However we might want to solve the problem of translation, the historical fact is that the Greek translation suggests strongly that what philosophers sought under the name of Being is basically identical with the God of the Hebrew covenant. If that is the case, it is not hard to see this biblical text as warrant for a larger theological project that envisions a very close bond between philosophy and theology. In fact, much of Western Christian theology reflects something of this conviction throughout its history.

Alfred North Whitehead once described Christianity as "a religion seeking a metaphysic" (*Religion in the Making* [New York: World Publishing Co., 1969], 50). In this sense, Whitehead contrasts Christianity with other religions which may be essentially either metaphysical or ethical systems. The description of Christianity as a religion in search of a proper metaphysical self-understanding is an apt summation of much of the actual history of Christian thought. During the centuries, Christianity has associated itself with philosophical and metaphysical modes of thought from the early second century onward. But the history of theology makes it clear that Christianity has never been able to espouse a particular philosophy or a metaphysical vision without subjecting that philosophy to critique and transformation.

This might be of considerable help when we turn to Bonaventure, as he tells us that the two cherubim above the ark symbolize two ways of contemplating the invisible mystery of God. The first way, turning to the name of God found in the Hebrew Scriptures and philosophy, focuses on what philosophy and philosophical theology know as the essential attributes of the divine in terms of its nature as primal unity, while the second way, turning to the name of God drawn from the Christian Scriptures, focuses on that which pertains properly to the divine persons of the Trinity.

The first way fixes the attention of the soul principally and first of all on Being Itself, proclaiming that the primary name of God is *The One Who is.* The second way turns the attention of the soul on the *Good Itself,* proclaiming that this is the primary name of God. (*JS* 5.2 [5:308])

As we move into Bonaventure's meditation, it might be helpful to keep in mind that puzzling question that seems to lie at the foundation of so much philosophical reflection. If everything we encounter in this world including ourselves is here today while it was not here at some point in the past, and it will not be here at some point in the future, why is it here at all? If everything seems to be profoundly contingent in that sense, then why is there anything at all when nothing we encounter needs to be? In more personal terms, each of us could ask: Why am I when I might not have been at all had circumstances in the life of my parents been even minimally different at the time of my conception?

Why is there anything when nothing that we experience empirically seems to be necessary? Just to hear that question seriously will help us to understand why the philosophers of antiquity could reach the conclusion that if contingent things exist, then somewhere there must be something that exists necessarily, for even an endless chain of contingent things really does not answer the question. It simply prolongs contingence.

Such a question is not just one for ancient philosophers. It is one that many people ask about their world or about themselves at particular times in their life. It is also one that contemporary cosmologists frequently ask at some point in their cosmological speculations. Thus, it seems to appear at the end of Stephen Hawking's *Brief History of Time* ([New York: Bantam Books, 1988], 175), where he looks to a time when science will have said all there is to say about what the cosmos is and how it works, and all people of good will can reflect together on this question: Why? And when they find an answer to the question why the universe exists at all, they will have come to know the mind of God. It appears in another form in the statement that E. Tryon gave when he was asked about the origins of the cosmos. "It's just one of those things that happen from time to time" (see A. Guth, *The Inflationary Universe: The Quest for a New Theory of Cosmic Origins* [Reading, Mass.: Addison-Wesley, 1997], 14).

The mystery of being: Why is there something rather than nothing? If everything in our experience seems to be contingent, does this mean that there must be something that exists necessarily? And if that is the case, does that mean that something of the necessary being might be intimated in our experience of contingence? This might be a helpful springboard for moving into

Bonaventure's meditation on God in terms of the metaphysical mystery of Being.

Anyone who wishes to contemplate the invisible things of God with respect to the unity of essence should first be attentive to Being itself, and see that Being itself is so completely certain that it cannot be thought not to be. The reason for this is that the thought of the most pure Being Itself would never enter our mind except in contrast with the thought of non-being, just as the idea of nothing stands in total contrast to the idea of being. Therefore, just as absolute nothingness contains not a shred of being, and none of the conditions of being, so by way of contrast, Being Itself possesses nothing of non-being, neither in act nor in potency, neither in its own reality, nor in our understanding of it. (*JS* 5.3 [5:308])

The analysis of Bonaventure moves in the direction of claiming that in the final analysis, when we have tried to give an account of our puzzling experience and our awe before the fact of existence, being is, in fact, that which comes first into the mind in this experience. The concept of being is at least implicit in every judgment we make about the existence of all the things we experience, even though we might not be aware of it. And the being we are speaking of, finally, is the divine Being. Yet it is difficult to recognize this to be the case.

How strange, then, is the blindness of the intellect which does not consider that which it sees first, and without which it would be impossible to know anything. (*JS* 5.4 [5:308])

At this point, Bonaventure employs the metaphor of light to provide some insight into what he is trying to say. Basically he claims that it is the mystery of the divine Being shining on our experience of the beings of this world that enables us to know them at all. We might compare this to the physical experience of light. It is the light of the sun that illumines the objects of our empirical experience enabling our eyes to see what is there. Light is the medium in which we see whatever it is that we see. However, if I were to turn my eyes away from the specific objects to look at the light itself, I would, in fact, seem to see nothing but empty space. And if I were to be very brave and turn to look at the source of the light, the sun would blind me. The light would be experienced as darkness. Bonaventure, following the lead of Aristotle, refers at this point to the example of the blindness of the bat to make his point.

Hence, it seems to be very true that "just as the eye of the bat is related to the light, so the eye of our mind is related to those things which are most manifest in nature." So, accustomed as it is to the darkness of beings and the phantasms of sensible objects, the eye of the mind seems to see nothing when it looks upon the light of the highest Being. It fails to understand that this darkness itself is the supreme illumination of the mind, just as when the eye looks at pure light it seems to itself that it sees nothing. (*JS* 5.4 [5:308])

If Being is involved in every experience we have of beings in this way, and if Being is to be identified with God, does this not mean that in some way God is involved in every experience we have of beings in the world? We never see God precisely as God, and when we turn to look at the divine light that makes our experience possible we seem to see nothing. But God is involved nonetheless.

Elsewhere in his more academic writings, Bonventure had argued that, in a certain sense, the existence of God is self-evident. It is impossible to formulate the judgment that affirms the nonexistence of God without being involved in a massive contradiction. The reflections we have just dealt with might shed light on the sort of logic involved here.

The existence of God is self-evident not in the sense that we have a vision of the divine essence, but in the sense that if we truly understand the proper meaning of the term *God,* whose primary name is Being, it is impossible to deny the existence of God with any logical cogency. In everything you know, you know something of God's existence without necessarily knowing that it is God that you are involved with.

You may deny the existence of God because you do not have

a proper understanding of the meaning of that name. Or you may deny God's existence for moral reasons, because you do not wish to live with the ethical implications of such a reality. But in the deepest level of human consciousness, it is impossible not to have some awareness of the divine. Our yearning for truth, goodness, beauty, and happiness together with our awareness of our own limitations cry out for the existence of that supreme Truth, Goodness, and Beauty which is God.

The truth of God's existence, then, is a truth that arises from the existence of every creature and is naturally imprinted on the human mind. The universe is filled with God; every creature proclaims the existence of the divine. The existence of God is so evident to the soul through reflection on itself that our reflection on the external world serves principally to remind us of that which we already know within. There is, then, an implicit awareness in human consciousness that can be made explicit through reflection on the implications of human experience.

Therefore, Bonaventure will argue that such things as proofs for the existence of God might best be understood as a form of spiritual exercise. They do not provide us with a new object of knowledge of which we had no prior awareness. Rather, they enable us to understand better the nature of the judgment that is involved when we affirm God's existence (*Trin.* 1.1 [5:45–51]).

After his moving meditation on God as Being, Bonaventure goes on to draw out the attributes of God when the divine mystery is viewed in terms of the unity of essence. Such a Being must be pure being, simple being, and absolute being. It must, therefore, be first, eternal, supremely simple, actual, most perfect, and supremely one. These he presents in a number of thought-provoking contrasts or opposites in a paradoxical style that comes to a high point when he reaches to the *Theological Rules* (rule 7) of Alan of Lille for the following description of God. God is "an intelligible sphere, whose center is everywhere and whose circumference is nowhere" (*JS* 5.8 [5:310]). Such a paradoxical juxtaposition of opposites pushes our mind even further than the opposites that have preceded it. Such a metaphysical reflection leads us in yet another way to a sense of awe and wonder at the mystery of our cosmos and even more at the mystery of Being in which it is grounded.

God, the Highest Good

In 1991, a book by the French author Jean-Luc Marion appeared in English translation. The title of this very challenging book is *God Without Being*. A part of the argument in the book has to do with the critique of the centuries-old metaphysical tradition that has conditioned at least Western Christians to think of God as the ultimate mystery of Being. We have just seen at least one version of that tradition above.

Two things stand out in Marion's argument. The first is the problem involved in the human tendency to create idols in place of the mystery of the divine. Idols can be in many forms. Some of them take the form of very concrete images of God which are too easily taken to be literal descriptions of the divine. Others are more rarified and difficult to recognize. These take the form of conceptual images and names for the divine that tend to be more abstract and are less likely to be seen in their limited nature. The second thing that stands out in Marion's argument is the claim that we need to take up seriously the possibility of approaching the mystery of the divine more emphatically in terms of the Christian claim that "God is love."

It is hard to read this very contemporary book and not be reminded of the vision of Bonaventure and the move he makes from his metaphysical meditation on God as Being, which we have just discussed, to the next level, the meditation on the specifically Christian name for God: God is the Good. As we have seen in the preceding section of this chapter, when God is viewed from the perspective of philosophy, or from that of the Hebrew Scriptures, specifically with the text of Exodus 3:14 in mind, it appears that the most basic name for God is simply Being. At least, that is our suspicion if we read this text in the Greek translation of the Septuagint rather than in the original language which was Hebrew. And so it was read for centuries, at least by Christians. But when we look at Bonaventure's meditation, we find that:

When Christ, our Master, wished to lead the young man who had observed the Law to the greater perfection of the Gospel, he named God principally and exclusively with the name of *Goodness.* He says: "No one is good but God alone." Hence, St. John Damascene, following Moses, says that *The One who is* is the first name of God. Dionysius, on the other hand, following Christ, says that *Good* is the first name of God. (*JS* 5.2 [5:308])

Were Bonaventure to pick up the book of Marion, he might be puzzled by the title. Why does the title say God *without* Being? Why does it not say God *beyond* Being? For to name God as Being is not incorrect in every sense of the term. For God is truly Being, Bonaventure would say. It becomes problematic, however, if you choose to stop there and say nothing further.

The philosophical understanding of a sort of self-enclosed, monadic Being is simply not adequate for the naming of God. Both the history of philosophy and the history of revelation in the Hebrew Scriptures must be held open to yet another level of insight. The primal level of Being is Being as the Good, or Loving Being. God, therefore, is not monadic, self-enclosed, unrelated substance. On the contrary, God is a mystery of primal, loving communion and relationality.

Thus, Bonaventure envisions two ways of reflecting on the mystery of the invisible God. These two ways, as we have seen, are symbolized by the two angelic figures facing each other on the top of the ark of the covenant in the Holy of Holies. We have already seen the impressive meditation on the mystery of Being symbolized by one of the angels. Now Bonaventure leads us into a consideration of the Christian vision of God as the primal mystery of the Good symbolized by the other angel.

What follows at this point is not simple theology. It is highly philosophical theology that reaches not only to the Scriptures, which, as we have just seen, name God as the Good, but to the

Neoplatonic philosophy of the good, which functions as a means of interpreting the implications of the biblical name.

From the Neoplatonic tradition, through Dionysius, Bonaventure borrows the language of self-diffusion. It is the nature of the good to be self-diffusive. But, if God is the highest Good, then God must be self-diffusive in the highest sense. To speak of a highest Good that could not be self-diffusive in the highest degree would simply be a contradiction.

Therefore, if God is the highest good, God must be supremely self-diffusive. But the supreme self-diffusiveness of the infinite God cannot be directed to creation, for then creation would, of necessity, be equal to God; it would, in fact, be divine. But this is impossible unless one is willing to envision some form of pantheism. That Bonaventure is not willing to do. It follows, then, that God must be supremely self-diffusive in a way that is internal to the mystery of the divinity itself, prior to and independent of any talk of creation. In essence, this is what Christian theology understands to be the mystery of the Trinity.

It was above all the work of Richard of St. Victor in the twelfth century that succeeded in reinterpreting the Neoplatonic tradition of the good from a Christian perspective that made it possible to speak of God's self-diffusion in the language of free and loving self-communication. Without making any explicit appeal to the Johannine way of naming God as *love* (1 John 4:8, 16) at this point in *The Journey of the Soul into God*, Bonaventure draws on the Victorine argument to make his point.

The argument revolves around an analysis of the nature of love. If God is the highest Good, and the nature of the highest Good is to be found in the highest form of love, then the mystery of the Trinity becomes the mystery of the primordial, self-communicative love which is productive within the Godhead before it moves outside to create the universe.

So it is that, out of these varied resources, Bonaventure crafts for us a vision of the divine as purest, loving, self-communicative Being. Internally, God is the purest loving self-communication. This is the point of the doctrine of the Trinity. In Bonaventure's view, if we wish to see God not simply as Being but as supreme Good, then we are well on the way to saying that there must be some plurality of persons in God. The Victorine and Bonaventurean arguments revolve around the analysis of different modes of love; and this analysis is based on centuries of Christian experience in attempting to live the meaning of the Christian vision of God in the context of human life. The argument runs along the following line.

There is such a thing as love of oneself, or private love, in the language of Richard of St. Victor. But this form of love can too easily become simply the highest form of narcissistic self-concern. It is better if one has love for another and not simply for oneself. And if that is the case, and God is to be thought of as love in the highest sense, then there must be at least two persons in God. The love between two persons is better than simple self-love. But, to move one step further, the desire of two persons deeply in love to share their love with another is even more noble than keeping it to themselves.

Hence, moving in this direction, both Richard and Bonaventure will argue that the theology of the Trinity is a necessary explication of the way God is named in the Christian Scriptures. It says basically that God is a mystery of primordial, loving communion. And love is self-diffusive or self-communicative. But, precisely because God is perfectly self-diffusive internally, God is free to be diffusive externally. It is precisely for this reason that Bonventure can see God's creative action purely and simply as an action of free, generous love. It is against this background that we must read the text of *The Journey of the Soul into God:*

For "the good is said to be self-diffusive." Therefore the highest good must be supremely self-diffusive. But the supreme self-diffusion cannot be unless it is actual and intrinsic, substantial and hypostatic, natural and voluntary, free and necessary, lacking in no way and perfect. Therefore, unless in the supreme good there is from eternity a production that is actual and consubstantial, and a hypostasis that is as noble as the producer, as is found in the case of a production by way of generation and spiration—so that what is from the eternal principle is also eternally from the co-principle—so that there is a beloved and a co-beloved, one generated and one spirated; that is Father, and Son, and Holy Spirit, in no way would this be the highest good, for it would not be supremely diffusive. For the diffusion in time in the form of creation is no more than a center or a point when compared with the immensity of the eternal good. From this, then, another greater self-diffusion can be thought of, namely, one in which the One who is diffusive communicates the whole of its substance and nature to another. And such a One would not be the highest good if it lacked the ability to do this in reality, or even in thought. (*JS* 6.2 [5:310])

In no way can creation be the eternal, perfect self-communication of God. But if God is already perfect self-communication independent of creation, then that self-diffusion in time which constitutes creation can be supremely free and totally uncoerced. Neither Plato nor Aristotle ever came to an understanding of the origin of the world in terms similar to the Christian doctrine of creation. This might be related to the fact that neither of them came to the idea that the most primal reality was, in fact, best thought of in terms of personal, loving, self-communicative goodness.

Plato might have sensed a hint of this in his notion of the highest Good. As Whitehead put it: "Can there by any doubt that the power of Christianity lies in its revelation in act, of that which Plato divined in theory?" (*Adventures of Ideas* [New York: Free Press, 1967], 167). Whatever one might say about Plato, Aristotle's prime mover seems quite far removed from a loving creator; and in fact, in Aristotle's philosophy, the prime mover does not create the world from nothing. Aristotle's world exists of necessity and from eternity. Bonaventure's world exists contingently and in time that has a beginning and will have an end. It exists simply because of the loving, creative will of God.

For Bonaventure, the Christian experience of the divine centered in the life and history of Jesus opens our eyes to a new way of thinking of God as well as the origin of our world and ourselves. Precisely because God is supreme love within the Godhead, God does not need to have a world in order to be God.

If there is a world, therefore, it is not because God must create. God, who is the purest of love within, creates not out of any need, but out of pure love so as to manifest something of the mystery of the divine truth, goodness, and beauty outwardly, and to bring forth creatures capable of participating in the splendor of the divine life thus conceived. And, grand as the cosmos appears to be from our perspective, Bonaventure writes, as we have just seen, that "creation is no more than a center or a point when compared with the immensity of the eternal good" (*JS* 6.2 [5:310]).

In his meditation on the mystery of the divine Trinity of loving being, Bonaventure invites us to an even greater sense of awe at the way in which the qualities of being are opened up to new levels of meaning and are held together in a sort of coincidence of opposites. Bonaventure alerts us to the mystery in the following words:

Do not think that you are able to understand the incomprehensible.... And yet, who would not be moved to greater wonder.... For when you consider these things one at a time, you have the basis for contemplating the truth; when you see them in relation with one another, you have something that will lift you up in the highest wonder. Therefore you should consider all these things together so that your mind might ascend in wonder to admirable contemplation. (*JS* 6.3 [5:311])

There can be little doubt that, for Bonaventure, the religious experience involved in the person and history of Jesus leads him not to reject philosophical metaphysics but to hold it open to yet further depths of meaning, and perhaps to significant correction. The doctrine of the Trinity is, in Bonaventure's eyes, clearly a correction of Aristotle's metaphysics that has major implications for our understanding of the created world in which we live. Hence, what we suggested at the opening of this section seems to flow from Bonaventure's reflections. If this is a fair reading of the text of *The Journey of the Soul into God,* we might describe Bonaventure's reflection as a meditation on the mystery of God *beyond* Being to a reflection on Being precisely as a Being-in-love. And when we follow Bonaventure on this way, we discover something that

leads the eye of the mind with great power to a stupor of awe. For there is the greatest communicability together with individuality of persons, the greatest consubstantiality together with plurality of hypostases, the greatest configurability together with distinct personality, the greatest co-equality together with order, the greatest co-eternity together with emanation, the greatest mutual intimacy together with mission of persons. Who would not be lifted to a sense of wonder at such great things? (*JS* 6.3 [5:311])

We notice how our ability to think and to speak about the mystery of God is being stretched in paradoxical ways. This must say something about any attempt of humans to name the mystery that remains always ineffable in its deepest reality. Not only is all philosophical language about the ultimate mystery seriously limited, so also is the language that Christians use to speak about the God of biblical revelation.

None of these images, metaphors, or concepts is to be taken as a literal description of God. Yet the clash of metaphors and the paradoxical sense that emerges from them open us to a deeper sense of mystery. We think of the statement of St. Augustine, who was keenly aware of the limits of every human attempt to name the divine. Finally, he says, we continue to speak about God so that our silence will not be construed as atheism.

At this stage of our journey with Bonaventure, we are still talking a lot. But we are saying very strange things. And eventually the Seraphic Doctor will lead us into silence. But before that, there is yet another dimension of the ark and the two cherubim to take into account. That is the point of our next chapter.

Chapter 5

Christ the Center

We have followed Bonaventure as he leads us ever more deeply into the temple, the mysterious symbol of divine presence: first in the outer court of the world and in our sense experience of the world; then in the inner court of the soul and in the transformation of the soul in grace; yet deeper into the temple through contemplation of two mysterious names for the divine, each represented symbolically by one of the angelic figures. Their wings overshadow the mercy-seat—that point in the temple at which the mystery of the divine presence is most sharply focused.

Now we approach the final stages of the journey. In the very depths of the temple, in that most sacred of all spots, at the mercy-seat, we encounter the mystery of Christ. For it is here in Bonaventure's text that we find the symbol that elicits an awareness of the "most marvelous union of God and humanity, in the unity of the person of Christ" (*JS* 6.4 [5:311])

In the opening section of *The Journey of the Soul into God* Bonaventure had invited the reader "to groans of prayer through Christ crucified, in whose blood we are cleansed from the filth of our vices" (*JS* prol. 4 [5:296]). The figure of Christ is basic in Bonaventure's spirituality and theology. We have spoken above about the need for the soul to be re-formed, and we indicated something of the role of Christ there.

Bonaventure also speaks of Christ in the language of Dionysius as the Hierarch through whose action the human soul is hierarchized. As we have seen, this means that all the soul's functions are put in the right order within the person and in a proper relation to their objects.

Now it is the figure of Christ that moves into the very center of Bonaventure's reflections. Specifically, it is the figure of Christ on the cross. And this is the figure evoked by the mysterious symbol from the Alverna experience. A reading of Bonaventure's more systematic works together with the christological references scattered throughout *The Journey of the Soul into God* make it clear that in his framework it is the Incarnate Word who stands out as the basis on which an authentic spirituality will be built.

The Christ of Dogma

At one level, the reflections on Christ are reflections about the mystery of the incarnation in its dogmatic dimension. The reflections about the two names for God given in our previous chapter are here brought together with the understanding of Christ as the Incarnate Word. It is here that we arrive at one of those stunning formulations of Bonaventure:

[W]hen in Christ, the Son of God, who is by nature the image of the invisible God, our mind contemplates our humanity so wonderfully exalted and so ineffably united, and when it sees at one time in one Being the first and the last, the highest and the lowest, the circumference and the center, the Alpha and the Omega, the caused and the cause, the Creator and the creature, that is, the book written within and without, it reaches something perfect. It now arrives at the perfection of its illuminations on the sixth stage, as if with God on the sixth day. Now nothing further remains but the day of rest on which through transports of the mind its power of discernment finds rest "from all the work that it has done." (*JS* 6.7 [5:312])

We recall here the Christocentric character of the spirituality of St. Francis. The spirituality of Francis revolves around his discovery of a Christ different from what was common at his time. In his own personal experiences, Francis breaks from the Byzantine tone of the Christ images common even in the West, and reflected to some extent even in the crucifix of San Damiano. In that crucifix, even on the cross we encounter a Christ already moving to glory. St. Francis will center his piety much more around the reality of the humanity of Jesus and come to see him more and more as a brother and as one whose life was somehow to be imitated in one's personal journey.

We have already pointed out how Bonaventure moves from that Christocentric form of spirituality to a metaphysical vision that places Christ at the very center of creation and history. Bonaventure's understanding of the christological dogma begins already in the dogma of the Trinity. That person who is at the center of the Trinity is the person who mediates all of God's work in creation and in the history of salvation. When that central person becomes incarnate, he assumes his rightful place publicly as the center of creation and history.

Thus, Bonaventure is convinced that there is a universal center of meaning, and it is to that center that we are called in our spiritual journey. Not only is one's personal spiritual life to be centered on Christ, but to the degree that this takes place, one's personal center comes into more perfect harmony with the center of reality—the center of the world and the very center of God. For Bonaventure, Christ is simply the universal center.

In laying out his plan for the *Collations on the Six Days of Creation*, Bonaventure writes about the starting point:

It is necessary to begin with the center, that is, with Christ. For He is the Mediator between God and humanity, holding the central position in all things, as will become clear. Therefore, it is necessary to begin with Him if a person wishes to reach Christian wisdom. . . . Our intention is to show that in Christ are "hidden all the treasures of wisdom and knowledge," and that He Himself is the central point of all knowledge. He is the central point in a sevenfold sense: namely, He is the center of essence, nature, distance, doctrine, moderation, justice, and concord. . . . Christ is the first center in His eternal generation, the second in His incarnation, the third in His passion, the fourth in His resurrection, the fifth in His ascension, the sixth in the judgment to come, the seventh in the eternal retribution or beatitude. (*SD* 1.10–11 [5:330–31])

Mysteries of the Life of Christ

Bonaventure at times virtually identifies the illuminative way with the spirituality of the imitation of Christ. One reason for this might be seen in his understanding of the symbolism of light. In many ways, the divine mystery itself can be seen under this symbol, and the action of God in human experience can be seen in terms of the diffusion of light. The mystery of God and God's grace illumines the human soul and lifts it up beyond itself much as the light of the sun reaches down to pick up water from the earth and lift it up to the sky. Insofar as Christ is the divine Word incarnate, his salvific work can be expressed in terms of the same symbolism. Thus, in his *Collations on the Six Days of Creation* Bonaventure writes:

In the allegorical sense, the sun signifies Christ. The sun rises, and the sun sets. It rises in His birth, it sets in His death; it circles through midday in His ascension; it is inclined to the north in the time of judgment. (*SD* 13.26 [5:391])

For Bonaventure, it is clear that not everything that Christ did during his earthly life is to be imitated by his followers. He distinguishes between instruction and imitation. It is true that everything in the life of Christ is for our instruction in some way. But not everything is for our imitation. Some of Christ's actions reveal the mystery of his divinity. Therefore, they instruct us; but it would be unwarranted pride to desire to imitate them. What we are called to imitate can be named in terms of the virtues that stand out in the history of Christ: humility, poverty, obedience, and charity.

So, a great number of actions shine from Christ who is the exemplar and origin of our entire salvation. Now some of these actions relate to His exalted power. These include walking on the water, transforming the elements [water into wine at Cana], multiplying the loaves, transfiguring Himself, and other miracles. Other actions relate to the light of wisdom. These refer to heavenly secrets, reading the secrets of hearts, and predicting future events. Other actions relate to the severity of judgment. These include casting the merchants from the temple, overturning the tables of those who were selling doves, and reproaching the priests severely. Other actions relate to the dignity of office. These include confecting the sacrament of His most holy body, the imposition of hands, and the forgiveness of sins. Other actions relate to the condescension of mercy. These include such things as hiding at the time of persecution, being fearful and sorrowful in the face of death, and praying to the Father to remove this chalice. Other actions relate to the form of the life of perfection. These include the observance of poverty, chastity, and obedience to God and to human beings, spending the night in prayer, praying for those who crucified Him, and offering Himself in death for his enemies out of supreme love. Thus, while there are six different forms of action, perfection consists in the imitation only of the last kind. (*DM* 2.13 [8:243])

So it is that Bonaventure, following the inspiration of St. Francis, attempts to clarify in greater detail what it is in the life of Christ that is for our imitation. This might help us to understand why it is that in many of Bonaventure's other writings, the emphasis is not so much on the theology of the hypostatic union; but, presupposing that, the emphasis will be on the mysteries of the life of Christ.

For Bonaventure, the human reality of Jesus and his history provide the historical base from which Christians derive their most fundamental insights into the mystery of God, of human nature, and of the world in which human beings find themselves. It is understandable, then, that Bonventure can lead us into moving meditations on all the mysteries of the life of Christ, from the annunciation all the way to the end of Jesus' history. The historical life of the Incarnate Word takes on archetypal significance as the historical, symbolic expression of the mystery of the eternal Word who lies at the very center of the Trinity.

It is through meditation on the mysteries of his life that we become more aware of the meaning of the eternal Word, and it is in the living out of the values of that historical life that we come into fuller harmony with the eternal archetype enfleshed in Jesus.

Ewert Cousins has suggested that we might see Bonaventure's work in this area as a mysticism of historical event. It is a way of drawing one into the dynamic of a historical situation, almost as a participant in the event, so as to be drawn into its deeper religious significance. Bonaventure's *Tree of Life, Mystical Vine,* and many of his sermons might serve well as examples of what is involved here.

In one of his sermons for the feast of the Epiphany, Bonaventure recalls the prophets Jeremiah and Hosea, who compare the relation of God with Israel to that of a husband with an unfaithful wife. Both of these prophets describe the return of the wife to the loving husband. This now serves as a way of viewing the return of the soul to Christ.

This is what the soul does when it recalls its spouse, our Lord Jesus Christ, who—for love of you—was born, lived, died, etc. Who would not love Him if one only recalled what He has done for us in His flesh? But it is necessary to turn back to Him frequently. A ray of the sun does little to warm things by simply passing over, but rather by lingering. In a similar way, a single thought, or recalling God but once, will hardly inflame the heart. Rather, we need to do this frequently. (*Sermon 4 on Epiph.* [9:162])

It is in this area that Bonaventure reveals a significant influence of the work of Bernard of Clairvaux. Particularly in his reflections on the *Canticle of Canticles,* the Cistercian had developed the spousal imagery of the biblical text as a way of emphasizing the relation of love that should develop between the soul and the person of Christ.

Bernard writes: "Learn from Christ Himself how you ought to love Christ, O Christian soul. Love sweetly, prudently, and intensely. Love sweetly, so that, in the light of His love, every other love will seem poor to you, and that Christ alone will be honey to your mouth, music to your ears, and joy to your heart. Love prudently, so that, without ceasing, your love will burn for Him and for no one else. Love intensely, so that your frailty will joyfully endure every hardship and pain for His sake, and that you may come to say: My trials lasted hardly an hour, and even if they were to last longer, because of love I would not feel them. This is how the Christian should always strive toward Christ through love: in such a way that he or she willingly supports any adversity until finally reaching Him." These are the words of Bernard. (*Solil.* 1.4, 43 [8:42])

Similar themes appear in the treatment of the sacrament of the Eucharist in the *Breviloquium:*

In a similar way, since it is in harmony with the time of grace that the sacrament of union and love not only signify this union and love, but also that it be a means of inflaming the heart in that direction so as to bring about what it represents. Because what most inflames us toward mutual love and what chiefly unites the members is the oneness of the Head from whom flows a mutual affection through a stream of love that pours forth, unites, and transforms, therefore this sacrament contains the true body and immaculate flesh of Christ in such a way that it pours into us, unites us to one another, and transforms us into Him through that most burning love by which He gave Himself to us, offered Himself up for us, and now returns to us and remains with us until the end of the world. (*Brevil.* 6.3 [5:254])

There can be little doubt that Bonaventure saw the possibility that reflection on the mysteries of Christ's life could lead one to the most exalted form of mystical experience. This, in fact, is what happened in the case in St. Francis on Mount Alverna.

The Cross

In this context, we must recall specifically the role that the cross of Christ played in the spirituality of St. Francis, beginning with the experience before the cross in the little church of San Damiano and reaching a climactic point in the experience of Alverna, when the wounds of the crucified Christ were imprinted in his own body.

When we think of Bonaventure's earlier reflection on the mystery of God in relation to the glories of nature, the focus seems to be on the greatness of God and the divine transcendence beyond the world of created realities. But, even at that level, we need to recall how St. Francis saw also the small, humble creatures as symbols of the divine. Both dimensions are present, though we easily move to greatness and glory.

When we look at the mystery of Christ, however, both for St. Francis and for Bonaventure, this evokes quite a different sense of the divine. When we think of the historical origins of Jesus, the poor circumstances of his life, the tragic historical ending on the cross, we must ask in what sense this is truly the incarnation of divine love. For both St. Francis and for Bonaventure, such historical realities point our attention to the humble, tender elements of the world in order to discover there important signals of the presence of the divine. How can one look at the figure on the cross without asking: What is the nature of creative and redemptive love? What is truly creative power?

Bonaventure himself will speak of the transformative power of love. It is a common human experience that a person is gradually changed by the persons or things that are most important in his or her life. We can see this at various levels. Married people who have struggled and worked and loved over many years are changed by that process. Relations between children and parents often reflect the same dynamic, as do many other types of relation. We are changed by those persons and things that enter deeply into our lives. And in a real sense, we become like what we love.

If this is true of human relations, may it not also be true of the relation between the human person and God? The life of grace and the imitation of Christ are a process of responding to the divine offer and the example of Christ. And the human person is changed in that process. We become like what we love. And if it is the divine, self-sacrificing love embodied in the figure on the cross that we truly love, we will become human beings who truly reflect such love in the world of human relations. Speaking of the peace that the human soul seeks, Bonaventure writes:

The road to this peace is through the most ardent love of the Crucified, the sort of love that so transformed Paul into Christ . . . that he declared: "With Christ I am nailed to the cross. It is now no longer I that live, but Christ lives in me." And this love so absorbed the soul of Francis that his spirit shone through his flesh the last two years of his life when he bore the most holy marks of the Passion in his body. (*JS* prol. 3 [5:295])

It is not surprising, therefore, to find that Bonaventure gives great emphasis to the mystery of the passion and the cross in many of his writings.

Woe to those who spend their entire lives studying logic, physics, or the principles of the sciences and who find nothing to savor in this knowledge. If they were to study the wood of the cross of Christ, they would find a knowledge there that is truly salvific. (*Sermon V on Second Sunday after Easter* [9:304])

In the prologue to the *Tree of Life,* Bonaventure writes as follows:

"With Christ I am nailed to the cross," says the second chapter of the Epistle to the Galatians. The true worshiper of God and the true disciple of Christ, wanting to be conformed perfectly to the Savior of all who was crucified for his sake, should try above all with close attention of the mind to carry the cross of Christ always both in soul and in body, until he can feel the truth of the apostle's words in himself. No one will have an affection or a lively experience of such a feeling unless, neither forgetting the Lord's passion nor being ungrateful for it, he contemplates—with vivid memory, penetrating mind, and loving will—the labors, the suffering, and the love of Jesus crucified, so that he can truthfully say with the bride: "A bundle of myrrh is my Beloved to me; He shall abide between my breasts." (*TL* prol. [8:68])

Later in the same work we read the following exhortation:

You who are redeemed, consider who He is, how great a person He is, and what sort of person He is who hangs on the cross for you. Consider whose death it is that gives life to the dead, and at whose passing the heavens and the earth mourn and the hard rocks are split asunder as if out of natural compassion. O human heart, you are hard with a hardness greater than that of any rock if at the recollection of such a great atonement you are not struck with terror, nor touched with compassion, nor torn with compunction, nor softened with piety. (*TL* 29 [8:79])

Another sort of meditation on the crucified Christ is found in the *Mystical Vine*, emphasizing the revelatory meaning of the wound in the side of Christ, and urging the reader to enter personally into that wound:

Your side was pierced in order that an entrance might be opened for us; Your heart was wounded so that we might dwell in that Vine free from all external tribulations. But Your heart was wounded also so that through the visible wound we might see the invisible wound of love. For one who loves ardently is wounded by love. How could this ardor be shown to us more effectively than by permitting not only His body but His very heart to be pierced with a lance? The wound of the flesh reveals the wound of the spirit. (*MV* 3.5 [8:164])

An entire chapter of *The Threefold Way* is given over to show the reader how it is that meditation on the suffering of Jesus and above all on the cross can lead by seven steps to the splendor of truth. These steps begin with the assent of faith to the mystery of the divinity of Christ who is suffering and move to a sense of empathy with him in his suffering and a sense of compassion for one's neighbor that reflects the love of Christ for humans which is enacted in His suffering. It culminates in the discovery of the most profound truths about God and the human condition, which Bonaventure describes as the splendor of truth. The chapter ends with the following:

This is how all is made known through the cross, since all things can be included in this sevenfold division. From this it follows that the cross is the key, the door, the way, and the very splendor of truth. Anyone who is willing to take up the cross and follow its way as we have described it will not walk in the darkness, but will have the light of life. (*TW* 3.3, 3 [8:12-14])

For Bonaventure, the mystery of the cross raises the question of renunciation and asceticism as an important dimension of the spiritual journey and of the imitation of Christ. It is found at perhaps its deepest level, as we have already seen, in his understanding of spiritual poverty. It plays a role also in various forms of meditation on the mysteries of the life of Christ, and it may be seen in a powerful form in the willingness to give oneself for the sake of the other in works of charity. Beyond this, it will involve also voluntary self-denial and mortification. Bonaventure offers a powerful statement of how he understands the mystery of the crucified Christ in relation to the spiritual life.

Therefore, my soul, with loving footsteps move close to Jesus wounded, to Jesus crowned with thorns, to Jesus fastened to the wood of the cross. With the apostle Thomas, do not only see in His hands the print of the nails, do not only put your finger into the place of the nails, do not only put your hand into His side, but enter with the whole of your being through the door of His side into the very heart of Jesus. There, transformed into Christ by the most burning love of the Crucified, pierced by the nails of the fear of God, wounded by the spear of heartfelt love, transfixed by the sword of intimate compassion, seek nothing, desire nothing, wish for no consolation other than to be able to die with Christ on the cross. Then you may cry out with the apostle Paul: "With Christ, I am nailed to the cross. It is now no longer I that live, but Christ lives in me." (*PL* 6.2 [8:120])

This text suggests, among other things, that the love one searches for in the spiritual journey, modeled after the love of Christ, is a loving compassion. The same tone appears in the following:

Finally, we should come to the most humble heart of Jesus most high through the open door of His side, pierced as it is with a lance. Here, beyond doubt, there lies hidden the treasure of that love which is desirable and ineffable. Here is found that devotion from which the grace of tears is drawn. Here we learn mildness and patience in our afflictions, and compassion for the afflicted. Here, above all, is found a "heart contrite and humbled." Such a great one desires your embraces; such a great one is waiting to embrace you. (*MV* 24.3 [8:189])

In the midst of this meditation stands the word *compassion*. In terms of its etymology, the word comes from the Latin *com-pati*. This verb means, literally, "to bear, to endure, or to suffer with." It names a love, then, that is willing to express itself in voluntary suffering for the good of others, as Christ has done. In this way, as Christ's human love in the service of God and humanity was a reflection of the mystery of the eternal Word, so the human love of the disciple of Christ will reflect the mystery of the eternal Word as the one who is totally from the Other, and totally at the service of the Other as it reaches to others. Meditation on the mystery of the cross should move one to a practical love of the crucified Christ which will express itself in the form of caring for others and in personal asceticism that takes its inspiration from the cross.

Already in his *Commentary on the Sentences,* Bonaventure refers back to the teaching of Gregory the Great to say:

Anyone who wishes to love God perfectly must first be concerned with the love of neighbor, just as one who wishes to become good as a contemplative must first be good in the active life, as Gregory teaches. (*III Sent.* d. 27, a. 2, q. 4 [8:610])

We might summarize Bonaventure's view by saying that the most basic signal of progress in the spiritual journey is the degree to which the human person becomes filled with the mystery of compassionate love, a love that reaches out to all things with a willingness to truly bear the weight of the other for the good of the other as Christ bore the weight of humanity even to the point of his cruel execution on the cross.

In *The Life of St. Francis* the Seraphic Doctor looks to the Saint of Assisi for an example of the relation between the active and the contemplative dimensions:

For he had learned wisely to divide the time given to him for gaining merit. Part of it he spent in working for his neighbor's salvation, and the other part he gave to the tranquil ecstasy of contemplation. Therefore when, according to the demands of time and place, he had given himself fully for the salvation of others, he would then leave behind the distraction of the crowds and seek out the secrets of solitude and a place of quiet where he could spend his time more freely with the Lord and cleanse himself of any dust that he might have picked up from his business with people. (*LM* 13.1 [8:542])

In these terms, Bonaventure describes the rhythms of the life of St. Francis immediately before the description of the experience of Alverna. Having brought us to this level of contemplation on the world, on ourselves, on God, and on the mystery of Christ, he now writes:

When the mind has done all of this, it must still, in beholding these things, transcend and pass over, not only this sensible world, but even itself. In this passing over, Christ is the way and the door; Christ is the ladder and the vehicle, like the mercy-seat above the ark of God and the "mystery that has been hidden from eternity." (*JS* 7.1 [5:312])

Here we stand before the very throne of God. We have done all it is in our power to do. It remains only to place ourselves fully in the loving embrace of God with Christ, to pass over into God. Here Bonaventure singles out St. Francis on Mount Alverna as the outstanding example of such a passing over. It is here that St. Francis becomes the perfect example of contemplation, as he had been the model of action earlier in his life. For Bonaventure, it is through the example of St. Francis that God invites all who would enter on the spiritual journey.

In a text filled with allusions to the experience of St. Francis on Mount Alverna and cast against the background of the Mosaic experience of the passage out of Egypt through the Red Sea, Bonaventure writes:

One who turns fully toward this mercy-seat and with faith, hope, and love, devotion, wonder, joy, appreciation, praise and rejoicing, beholds Christ hanging on the cross, such a one celebrates the Pasch, that is, the Passover, with Him. Thus, using the staff of the cross, such a person may pass over the Red Sea, going from Egypt into the desert, where he or she may taste the hidden manna; and with Christ may rest in the tomb, dead, as it were, to the outside world; but experiencing, nevertheless, as far as is possible in this present state as wayfarer, what was said on the cross to the thief who was hanging there with Christ: "This day you shall be with me in Paradise." (*JS* 7.2 [5:312])

Chapter 6

The Goal of the Journey

Already in the Prologue to *The Journey of the Soul into God* Bonaventure gives the reader some clues as to the outcome of the journey. He does this with his description of the vision of the seraph in the form of the Crucified which overwhelmed St. Francis on Mount Alverna. Speaking of that experience, Bonaventure writes:

As I reflected on this it came to me immediately that this vision signified our Father's own suspension in contemplation as well as the way through which one arrives at that state. (*JS* prol. 2 [5:295])

We will now reflect on the meaning of this in the broader context of Bonaventure's program.

In our introduction we spoke of Bonaventure's work as a case of what is known as wisdom theology. As we come to the end of his analysis and look to the goal that he opens before us, we can see more clearly what this meant to him. We have already indicated that, in his view, while knowledge could be an important dimension of the human, spiritual journey, it is not the goal of that journey but a step on the way to the goal. The goal itself, as we have indicated, is best described in the language of a love that draws one beyond mere cognition.

While Bonaventure can speak of a certain form of wisdom already at the level of philosophy, that sort of wisdom is the fruit of human effort. At this level, it can include our basic knowledge of reality. More specifically, it can be taken to mean a more sophisticated kind of knowledge such as we find in philosophical metaphysics. This is a sort of knowledge which truly strives to see things in terms of their fundamental causes.

So, in Bonaventure's understanding, wisdom is not a simple, univocal term. There are levels of wisdom that seem to be the fruit of human effort and ingenuity. But the highest form of wisdom, which is our present concern, is not won through such work. It is a gift of the Holy Spirit and is probably best understood to be a form of what later authors will call infused contemplation.

O soul, great is that which you desire, and priceless is the gift you wish for so eagerly. But it cannot be obtained by human effort; it cannot be earned by human merit. It might be received from God through the humble prayer of a well-disposed soul, but only because of God's divine and merciful condescension. "For all gold, in view of it, is but a bit of sand, and before it silver is to be accounted as nothing." (*Solil.* 2.3, 14 [8:50])

As a youthful commentator on the *Sentences* of Lombard, Bonaventure had written that in the most proper sense the word *wisdom*

designates an experiential knowledge of God; and in this sense, it is one of the seven gifts of the Holy Spirit. The act of this gift consists in tasting the divine sweetness. . . . The act of the gift of wisdom is partly cognitive and partly affective. It begins in knowledge and is consummated in affection. The taste or savoring is an experiential knowledge of that which is good and sweet. . . . Such wisdom cannot be excessive, because excess in experiencing the divine sweetness is to be praised rather than to be condemned. Such a thing can be seen in holy and contemplative persons who at times are elevated to ecstasy because of the great sweetness, and at times are lifted up to rapture, though this happens to very few. It must be conceded, therefore, that the principal act of the gift of wisdom lies in the area of affect. (*III Sent.* d. 35, a. un., resp. [3:774])

Bonaventure speaks in similar terms in his treatment of the

various forms of knowledge of the divine, which he describes in a wide-ranging discussion of the experience of Adam in the state of innocence (*II Sent*. d. 23, a. 2, q. 3 [2:544]). In the context of this discussion, Bonaventure singles out the case of St. Paul, which he sees as involving a very special privilege. It is described in the language of rapture as an experience in which one does not act but rather is acted upon. It is a privilege reserved to very few. We assume, therefore, that rapture is not to be identified with the goal of the journey Bonaventure has been describing for us. This goal lies in the area of what he calls ecstasy, as we shall see.

In his final work, Bonaventure clearly distinguishes between ecstasy and rapture. The context for his discussion consists of a schema of seven levels of experience corresponding to the six days of creation followed by the seventh day of Sabbath rest. It is on the sixth day that God brings the work of creation to completion. If the number six is taken as symbolic of human history, and if the sixth day means some form of completion, it can be seen to symbolize that point toward the end of history—either individual history or collective history—when humanity reaches its fullest, historical maturity, immediately prior to the peace and rest of the seventh day.

Since the end of personal history means a passage through death, it involves the separation of the soul from the body, whereas the fullness of life in heaven will involve the reunion of soul and body. In medieval theology, this reunion is seen to take place at the end of the collective history of the human race.

The sixth day, therefore, can be taken to symbolize a high degree of maturity, in this case as seen in a very exalted form of experience. In this symbolic framework, Bonaventure suggests that there are levels of experience that can be thought of as similar to the passage through death to the vision of heaven. Such experiences can include both ecstasy and rapture. But ecstasy and rapture are not to be identified with each other. Ecstasy is a lesser form of experience, and is the more frequent of the two. Rapture, as Bonaventure understands it, is very rare. It seems to consist in a vision of God which, already here in history, anticipates the experience of the beatific vision. Bonaventure sees it as being involved in the experience of St. Paul, and he uses the work of Richard of St. Victor to express his view.

The text of Richard deals with the character of Issachar, one of Jacob's sons mentioned in Genesis 49. Issachar is described by Richard as living in the space between a land that he has to put up with by reason of necessity, and another land which he can see and which he desires for the sake of enjoyment (*The Twelve Patriarchs,* ch. 39). In this way Issachar can be seen as a symbol of a person standing at a limited place in history yet yearning for something greater that lies in the future.

Using this as the background for his reflections, Bonaventure seems to place this exalted experience of rapture at the boundary that distinguishes historical experience from heavenly experience. Or, we might say that a person standing within history enjoys an actual foretaste of heaven. Bonaventure puts it as follows:

The sixth vision is that of understanding absorbed by rapture into God. Hence, the Epistle to the Corinthians says: "I know a man in Christ who fourteen years ago—whether in the body or out of the body I do not know, God knows—such a one was caught up in this way." This lifting up makes the soul as similar to God as is possible within history. Ecstasy and rapture are not the same. Therefore it is said that they [who experience rapture] do not possess glory as a habit, but they do experience the act of glory. Thus this vision stands at the border between history and heaven, and at the border between the separation and union of soul and body. (*SD* 3.30 [5:347–48])

By way of contrast, in the same work, Bonaventure speaks of ecstasy in the following terms:

This contemplation comes about through grace, but human effort can be helpful; for it can separate the self from everything that is not God, and even from itself, if that is possible. And this is the highest union of love. And the Apostle says that it takes place only through love: "Being rooted and grounded in love so that you may comprehend with all the saints what is the length, the width, the height, and the depth." This love transcends all understanding and knowledge. But if it transcends knowledge, how can this wisdom be seen? This is why the Apostle continues: "Now to anyone who is able to realize all these things in a measure far beyond what we ask or conceive, etc." For it does not come to anyone but to the one to whom God reveals it. Therefore the Apostle says: "But to us God has revealed it by the Spirit." Since the mind is joined to God in this union, in one sense it sleeps, but in another sense it keeps vigil. "I sleep, but my heart is awake." It is only the affective power that keeps vigil, and it imposes silence on all the other powers. For this reason, a person is alienated from the senses, and—being placed in ecstasy—hears hidden things which a person is not allowed to speak, because they are affairs of the heart. Therefore, since nothing can be spoken unless it is first conceived, and nothing can be conceived unless it is first understood, the intellect remains silent. It follows that a person can hardly speak or explain anything. And so it is. Now, since no one arrives at such wisdom except through grace, a wise author looks to the Holy Spirit and to the Word himself to reveal all hidden and unforeseeable things. (*SD* 2.30 [5:341])

From here we can look at the final paragraphs of *The Journey of the Soul into God*, where Bonaventure speaks again of the experience that is the goal of the journey. The six days of creation are finished. There remains now the seventh day of Sabbath rest. At this point, Bonaventure speaks of the levels of reflection which we have followed with him as "steps to the true throne by which a person ascends to peace, where the truly peaceful person rests in peace of mind as if in an interior Jerusalem" (*JS* 7.1 [5:312]).

What has gone before has been, at best, a dark and obscure sense of the divine. But at this point, Bonaventure is inviting us to move yet further. The theme of peace is strong; the kind of inner peace that one experiences when one has reached a level of personal integration. This sense of integration or focusing is expressed in *The Threefold Way* in the following terms:

Finally, how are we to be concerned with the little flame of wisdom? We should move in the following order: this little flame is first to be concentrated, second it is to be nourished, third it is to be lifted up. It is concentrated by drawing our affections away from all love of creation. Since there is no advantage to be found in the love of creation, it is necessary that our affection be drawn away from this sort of love. If there is no advantage to be found in such love, then it does not refresh; and if it does not refresh, it does not satisfy us. Therefore, all love of this sort must be removed from our affection.

Second, it is to be nourished. This takes place by turning our affection to the love of the Spouse. We do this by considering love in relation to ourselves, to those in heaven, and to the Spouse Himself. The soul does this when it gives thought to the fact that every need can be filled by love, that because of love the full abundance of every good is in the blessed, and that through love one enjoys the presence of the One who is supremely desirable. These are the things that nourish our affections.

Third, it is to be lifted up beyond everything that can be sensed, imagined, or understood. This should be done in the following order. The soul should first meditate on the God whom it wishes to love perfectly, and it will see immediately that this God cannot be sensed, seen, heard, smelled, or tasted, and therefore is not an object of sense perception; and yet is totally desirable. Second, the soul should reflect on the fact that this God cannot be imagined because God has no limits, no figure, no number, no quantity, and no changeability, and therefore cannot be imagined, and yet is totally desirable. Third, the soul should reflect on the fact that this God is beyond our understanding, because God is beyond demonstration, definition, opinion, estimation, or investigation. So, this God is beyond our understanding and yet is totally desirable. (*TW* 1.15–17 [8:7])

In his final *Collations*, Bonaventure expresses it this way:

In this union, the power of the soul is drawn together and becomes more unified. The soul enters into its deepest self and consequently rises to its highest self. For according to Augustine, the deepest self and the highest self are identical.. . . But in order to reach such a condition, it is good for us to be carried above every sense experience, and above every rational operation related to the imagination. . . . And this is what Dionysius teaches: to dismiss sensible and intellectual things, beings and non-beings—and by non-beings he means temporal things because they are constantly undergoing change—and thus to enter into the radiance of darkness. It is called darkness because the intellect does not grasp it, and yet the soul is supremely illumined. (*SD* 2.31–32 [5:341–42])

Later in the same work, Bonaventure expresses his view on ecstatic contemplation, comparing the contemplative and active dimensions of human life to the moon, which waxes and wanes. Think of the church, and of the individual members of the church, as similar to the moon in its relation to the sun and its movements of waxing and waning. Those in the church militant are engaged in both active and contemplative concerns. When they are engaged in contemplation and draw closer to God as the moon approaches closer to the sun, they receive the fullest illumination; and when they are engaged in activity, their illumination decreases. There is no human being whose illumination is not diminished by action except Jesus Christ, who was perfect in both action and contemplation. When the contemplative person is most fully illumined, he or she frequently appears unusual or disfigured to others. Bonaventure then compares the soul to the hemisphere of the moon in the following words.

The moon which waxes and wanes signifies a person in the active and in the contemplative life. The morning star at times precedes the sun, and then it signifies the contemplative life. At other times it comes later than the sun. Then it signifies the active life. . . . As the bride is attracted to the groom . . . so the soul desires to be united through the ecstasies of contemplation. When the hemisphere of the soul is completely filled with light, then exteriorly the person seems to be entirely deformed and becomes speechless. Hence, these words of the *Canticle* contain a truth: "Do not stare at me if I am dark, because the sun has burned me," for then the soul is supremely conjoined with the interior illuminations. Hence, also, the words of Exodus: "Since You have spoken to Your servant, I am impeded more and slower of tongue." It was the same with Jacob, that is Israel. He was a strong man who was strengthened in his fight with the angel. Yet he dislocated the socket of his thigh, and he began to limp, because such contemplation makes the soul appear low to people when it is united with the supreme sun. (*SD* 20.18–19 [5:428–29])

How can one explain that the effect of the supreme illumination will be darkness and silence? To this Bonaventure writes:

Why is it that this radiation blinds when it should have enlightened? But this blinding is, in fact, the highest illumination because it occurs in the highest point of the mind, beyond the investigations of the human intellect. Here, the intellect is in darkness; it cannot investigate since the issue transcends every investigative power. There is only inaccessible darkness which nonetheless illumines those minds that have rid themselves of idle investigations. And that is what the Lord says, namely, that He dwells "in a cloud." And in the Psalms: "He made darkness the cloak about Him." (*SD* 20.11 [5:427])

Again, in the *Breviloquium*, after describing the various levels of human knowledge, Bonaventure brings his description to an end by mentioning wisdom. This he calls an ecstatic form of knowledge, which begins in this life and reaches its completion in the next life. He then describes the soul in its desire to be united with Christ, its Spouse.

In its most fervent desire, the soul not only becomes like a flame, quick to rise; it is even drawn up beyond itself into darkness and ecstasy through a certain learned ignorance. Wherefore the soul is not only able to say together with the bride, "We will run after you to the odor of your ointments," but it can also sing with the prophet: "Night shall be my light in my pleasures." Only one who has experienced the wonder of this obscure, delightful light can tell of it. No one can experience it unless it is given by divine grace. And only those who strive for it will receive such grace. (*Brevil.* 5.6 [5:260])

In *The Journey of the Soul into God* we find similar ideas. And here the language of mysticism and gift becomes very strong. The peace of which Bonaventure had spoken at the outset is now to be found by silencing all the cognitive activities of the soul, leaving behind all the images of the senses, entering into the darkness of a silence in which all our concerns are forgotten and in which, to some degree, God can be tasted. This tasting or savoring of God in mystical union is the peace which Bonaventure is seeking. In the prologue to *The Journey of the Soul into God,* Bonaventure writes:

To those who are already prepared by reason of divine grace, that is, to the humble and pious, to the repentant and devout, to those who are anointed with the oil of gladness, to those who love the divine wisdom and to those inflamed with a desire for it, to those who wish to give themselves to glorifying, admiring, and even tasting God—to such people I propose the following reflections, keeping in mind that the external mirror is of little or no significance unless the internal mirror of our mind is clear and polished. (*JS* prol. 4 [5:296])

The further implications of that become clear now at the end of the journey:

In this passing over, if it is to be perfect, all intellectual activities should be abandoned, and the most profound affections transported to God, and transformed into God. This, however, is mystical and most secret, which no one knows except one who receives it, and no one receives it except one who desires it, and no one desires it except one who is penetrated to the marrow by the fire of the Holy Spirit, Whom Christ has sent into the world. (*JS* 7.4 [5:312])

As we have seen above, Bonaventure is talking about an experience of a person who stands within history. It is here described as a very intense experience of loving, transforming union with God, which here comes to some level of awareness or consciousness. In the text we have just cited, Bonaventure seems to be speaking of a form of what later authors will call infused contemplation. This is not simply the fruit of human effort. One must receive it. All the intellectual activity is a prelude. But, eventually one moves beyond what is possible to human intelligence alone. The higher one goes in the journey, the greater is the need for grace. Eventually, it is purely a gift of God in the Holy Spirit.

And in making the spiritual journey Bonaventure has been describing, the christological dimension remains with us up to the end:

It [the soul] must still pass over, not only this sensible world, but even itself. In this passage, Christ is the way and the door; Christ is the ladder and the vehicle, being like the mercy-seat above the ark of God and like the mystery which has been hidden from eternity. (*JS* 7.1 [5:312])

We note here the remarkable convergence of symbols. That of the passage has been with us all along. It here comes together explicitly with that of the ladder to draw us to a sense of the goal of the journey. Specifically, here Christ is named as the way, the door, the ladder, and the vehicle. He is explicitly related to the mercy-seat. And all of this is unmistakably drawn into relation with the experience of St. Francis on Mount Alverna and with Bonaventure's experience on the same site.

This is what was made known to the Blessed Francis when, in an excess of contemplation on the height of the mountain—where I thought over the things which I have written here—there appeared a seraph with six wings fastened to a cross. I and many others have heard this from the companion who was with him there. It is here that he passed into God in an ecstasy of contemplation. And he became the example of perfect contemplation as previously he had been the example of action. . . . And so, through him God would invite all truly spiritual people to this kind of passing over and this ecstasy of soul, more by example than by word. (*JS* 7.3 [5:312])

Here Bonaventure reaches to Dionysius again, this time for the remarkable, paradoxical language which elicits an awareness of mystery without offering any clear image of God. He speaks of the

superluminous darkness of a silence, that teaches secretly in the greatest obscurity, that is manifest above all manifestations; of a darkness that is resplendent above all splendor, and in which everything shines forth; of a darkness which fills invisible intellects full above all fullness with the splendors of invisible goods that are above all good. (*JS* 7.5 [5:312–13])

It is an appeal, after all this activity on the journey, to leave behind all concern for sense experiences, and for all intellectual activities, so that

transcending yourself and all things, you might ascend to the superessential gleam of the divine darkness by an immeasurable and absolute ecstasy of a pure mind. (ibid.)

Language is here being pushed to its outer limits. Metaphors clash in the remarkable paradox of a darkness that is light. The Dionysian language of ecstasy appears here. And then the final silence.

At the end of his discussion of the human knowledge of Christ, the young Bonaventure had come to a similarly stunning conclusion:

It is only with great difficulty that this sort of knowledge can be understood. And it cannot be understood at all except by someone who has experienced it. And no one will experience it except a person who is "rooted and grounded in love so as to comprehend with all the saints what is the length and the breadth," etc. And this is what true, experiential wisdom consists in. It begins on earth and is brought to consummation in heaven. (*KC* [5:43])

The intensity of the experience stands out again. And Bonaventure describes it once more as an experiential wisdom. We might take that to mean some level of awareness of the union with God involved in grace. Over and over, we see Bonaventure reaching to Dionysius for comments on the peculiarity of language, moving from positive statements (it is like . . .) to negative statements (it is not like . . .) and then to superlative statements (it is more than . . .).

This movement in language is made not because what we are trying to express is false, but because the reality of the divine so thoroughly surpasses our ability to know and to speak that no human words can give an adequate expression to it. The experience of which Bonaventure speaks lies beyond all the knowledge we can derive from either our sense experience or our intellectual efforts. And therefore, finally, with Bonventure, we lapse into silence.

We could not wish for a more pointed statement of what is meant by the apophatic tradition in the literature of mysticism. When all has been said and done, finally the experience is incommunicable to anyone else. It may have remarkable power in the life of the person who experiences it. And, as Bonaventure indicates a number of times, another person who has had a similar experience will recognize something in what is said about it. But for a person who has never had such an experience, the language says nothing significant.

Whatever this experience might be, in Bonaventure's analysis, it seems fair to say that it is above all a gift of God to the human person, and that it lies beyond the categories of cognition. In the case of Bonaventure, that which draws us beyond cognition is the mystery of love. Drawn beyond itself by the magnetic attraction of the divine, the human person transcends itself in the direction of that divine love which has poured itself out in the figure of the man on the cross. Again, we stand with Francis and Bonaventure on the heights of Alverna.

Bonaventure is, therefore, pointing to the radically transformative power of a love that moves beyond mere knowledge. About this he writes in the *Soliloquy:*

O my soul, if you doubt and wonder at my words because they are the words of a sinner, then listen to Augustine, and listen to Paul. Behold, this is what Augustine says: "When we take hold of something eternal through knowledge and love, we are in spirit no longer on this earth." And the Apostle says: "But your citizenship is in heaven." O my soul, I think that you exist more truly "where you love than where you merely live," since "you are transformed into the likeness of whatever you love, through the power of this love itself." If you contemplate and love the things of heaven, how could you fail to live in heaven, for in your daily life you resemble the heavenly spirits? (*Solil.* 2.12 [8:49])

The journey that has taken us through so many different levels of consciousness and forms of knowledge now culminates in the love of that which the soul has discovered but cannot put into words with any degree of adequacy. So the contemplative person finally moves beyond all the cognitive processes—beyond cognition, beyond meditation, and finally to contemplation, sitting in silence in the presence of the inconceivable mystery of Absolute Love. After one has made every effort to express intellectually the mystery that draws the human spirit beyond itself, one finally ends those efforts and passes into the silence of a love that transcends any effort of intellectualization.

The discussion in *The Threefold Way* speaks of the unitive stage in similar terms. Coming to the end of a section on the steps involved in moving to the sweetness of love, Bonaventure writes:

The steps of the unitive way are distinguished as follows: watchfulness should arouse you, since the Spouse is near; confidence should strengthen you, since He is faithful; desire should inflame you, since He is sweet; rapture should lift you up, since He is exalted; delight should bring you peace, since He is beautiful; joy should inebriate you, because of the fullness of His love; closeness must unite you firmly to Him, because of the strength of His love. Therefore, the devout soul, in its depths, will always say to the Lord: It is You I seek; in You I hope; for You I long; to you I rise; You I receive; in You I exult; and to You I finally cling. (*TW* 3.5, 8 [8:15])

At the end of the *Soliloquy,* Bonaventure brings his reflections together in the form of a prayer.

I pray, my God, that I may know you; that I may love you; and that I may rejoice in you forever. And if I am not able to expe-

rience this to the fullest in this life, may at least my knowledge
and love of you increase in this life that my joy may be full in
the next life; that the joy which I here hold in hope may there
be brought to fulfillment. O Lord, our Father, you counseled, or
rather through your Son you commanded that we ask for this
fullness of joy; and you promised to hear our prayer. I ask of
you, O Lord, for that which, through your Wonder-Counselor,
you encouraged us to ask for and promised to grant: that our
joy may be full. Meanwhile, let my mind meditate on this joy;
let my tongue speak of it; let my heart desire it; let my words
extol it; let my soul hunger for it; let my flesh thirst for it; and
let my whole substance yearn for it, until I enter into the joy
of my God who is Three and One, blessed forever. Amen. (*Solil.*
4.27 [8:67])

We conclude that for Bonaventure, the spiritual journey is a
process of transformation which takes place under the power of
divine grace. Removing any obstacles that stand in the way of the
journey is the concern of the purgative way. This opens one to the
illuminative way, which, in Bonaventure's understanding, consists above all in the imitation of Christ. In essence, the illuminative way involves the basic remaking of oneself through the
integration of the various levels of one's experience and reshap-
ing oneself in the light of the virtues of Christ. Thus, the practice
of the virtues that flows from the personal integration is but the
expression of the inner imitation of God's love that has been
made manifest in Christ, which is so central to Bonaventure's
vision.

The illuminative way in the form of the imitation of Christ
leads us into a deeper experience of union with God. When
Bonaventure speaks of the highest levels of the contemplative
journey as an experiential knowledge, or an experiential wisdom,
he is speaking of a level that is inaccessible to our normal
processes of sensation and reasoning and which, therefore, lies
beyond our normal cognitive and volitional power. Yet he speaks
of it in the terminology of the spiritual senses. He speaks of taste,
smell, and delight.

Are these ways of saying that this mystical experience is not some sort of direct vision of the divine essence, but an interior sense that the soul is being touched in some mysterious way by the presence of the divine? Is this, then, the difference between ecstasy and rapture? Ecstasy is, above all, still an experience within history; it is still in darkness. Rapture, on the other hand, is described several times in terms of what contemporary theologians speak of as proleptic eschatology; it is a momentary, anticipatory experience of the act of glory.

An eloquent text in the *Collations on the Six Days of Creation* appeals to the *Canticle of Canticles* to speak of rapture as the soul's highest experience:

When the soul does what it is capable of doing, it is easy for grace to lift the soul up. . . . Then the soul is rapt in God, that is, in its beloved. Therefore, the Canticle says: "His left hand is under my head, and his right arm embraces me. I belong to my beloved, and my beloved belongs to me. He feeds among the lilies." For the soul already senses something of that union which makes it to be one spirit with God; as it is written: "One who clings to God is one spirit with God." And this is the supreme experience for the soul. It enables the soul to have a taste of heaven. (*SD* 22.39 [5:443])

We have exercised our mental powers to the fullest on the journey. We have thought; we have meditated; we have reasoned. We now sit in silence, in awe, totally captivated by the mystery of divine love which draws us. This level of experience is preeminently the gift of God's grace.

Note that this is the high point of Christian wisdom. Therefore, Dionysius, when he had written many books, stopped here, namely, in mystical theology. Therefore it is important that a person be instructed in many things, and in all of what has preceded. Concerning mystical theology, Dionysius has written: "But you, Timothy—my friend—concerning mystical vision, with strong action and contrition, give up the senses." He wants to say that it is necessary for a person to be freed of all those things which can be counted and to give them all up, as if saying the one I wish to understand is beyond all substance and knowledge. Here is an operation that transcends all knowledge. It is supremely secret, and no one knows it but one who has experienced it. In the soul there are a number of apprehensive powers: sensitive, imaginative, estimative, and intellective. It is necessary to leave all these; and at the summit there is a union of love that transcends all these. Therefore, it is clear that the fullness of beatitude is not found by the intellective power alone.

This contemplation takes place through grace, but human effort is of some help; for it separates the self from what is not God, and even from itself if that is possible. . . . Love of this sort transcends every intellect and every science. (*SD* 2.29–30 [5:341])

In *The Journey of the Soul into God*, the final metaphor Bonaventure uses to point in the direction of the divine is that of fire— a flame that ignites all it touches and burns white in the passion of Christ. As we come to the end of the journey with the Seraphic Doctor, he addresses us in the following eloquent words, which Evelyn Underhill describes as a "passage which all students of theology should ever keep in mind" (*Mysticism* [New York: Dutton, 1961], 124):

If you would like to know how these things come about, ask grace, not doctrine; desire, not understanding; the cry of prayer, not the labor of study; the Bridegroom, not the teacher; God, not a human person; darkness, not clarity; not light, but that fire which inflames totally and which will carry you into God with the greatest sweetness and the most burning affections. This fire, indeed, is God, and God's "furnace is in Jerusalem"; and it is Christ who enkindles it in the white flame of His most burning passion. This fire is truly perceived only by one who says: "My soul chooses hanging, and my bones, death." And one who loves this death can see God, for it is true without doubt that "no one shall see me and live."

Let us, then, die. And let us enter into this darkness. Let us silence all our cares, desires, and sense images. Let us pass over with Christ crucified from this world to the Father so that, when the Father is shown to us, we might say with Philip: "It is enough for us." Let us hear with Paul: "My grace is sufficient for you." Let us exult with David as we say: "My flesh and my heart waste away. You are the God of my heart and the God who is my portion for eternity. Blessed be the Lord forever. And let all people say: So let it be; so let it be. Amen." (*JS* 7.6 [5:313])

Conclusion

We have looked at some of the major texts of the Seraphic Doctor in the previous pages. We would now like to ask what wisdom this tradition might have to offer us today as we come to the beginning of a new millennium. Our concern is not simply to reconstruct a system from the past. Rather, now that we have searched through that system, we wish to highlight some insights that may be important for people of a very different time and place.

The metaphor of a spiritual journey is certainly not peculiar to Bonaventure, nor even to Christian spirituality. This metaphor, together with numerous related motifs, can be found widely in the world of religion. It might even be thought of as an archetypal metaphor. What is interesting in the work of Bonaventure is to see how this archetype is laid out so richly in specifically Christian insights into the nature of God, world, humanity, and Christ. It would be interesting to compare this with the way the metaphor is dealt with in other religious contexts. This might be a helpful point of departure for some form of conversation between the spirituality of diverse traditions. In this time of growing global consciousness, this could be a significant development in coming to understand in what ways the religious traditions resonate with one another, and what the deeper significance of their differences might be.

To some authors, the tone of Bonaventure's writing seems to be too much concerned with the spiritual development of individuals. Many would sense relatively little of the communal dimensions that seem to be of such concern today. And yet the view of Bonaventure does not isolate the individual from the community of the church. We have seen his words about the individual coming into greater conformity with the church militant, and we have seen some of his theology of the Eucharist, which is central to his understanding of the faith community. And we have heard him speak of compassionate love for others in the imitation of Christ. While a text such as *The Journey of the Soul into God* is concerned primarily with the journey of the individual person, the church is not absent even there. In the *Collations on the Six Days of Creation* Bonaventure presents a vision of the spiritual journey of the church itself, which is there described as the "contemplative church." Overall, it is true to say that, in Bonaventure's view, the spiritual journey is not that of an individual soul isolated from the world and from the church. It is, rather, the journey of the particular soul embedded in the context of the church and the world of God's creation. The dimension of the church and the human community is not absent from this spiritual vision, but it is not developed and made explicit to the extent that many would like to see it today. Above all, it is not developed in modern psychological terms.

But even though this may seem to be problematic for some, it is still important to recognize the significance of a spirituality that does not allow the individual to become swallowed up in some form of group ideology. When all is said and done, in the final analysis, the individual is responsible for his or her own life, even though that life cannot be lived effectively in isolation from the community. How to relate the personal and the communal dimensions is the real issue. Bonaventure offers important insights concerning the inner life of the individual which can well be drawn into a more explicit sense of community.

What we find here is a spiritual tradition that urges us to heighten our awareness of the nature and the dignity of the human person. There is something distinctive about human beings, and it does not help to say that this is not the case. It becomes important, then, that we learn to name what it is that makes us distinctive, and to realize that being distinctive does not mean that we are unrelated. When Bonaventure speaks of how the rest of creation is to serve us, what he has in mind primarily is the way in which it is able to awaken us to the mystery of God so that in human beings, the whole of creation finds an intelligent, free voice of praise to God.

Perhaps one of the great advantages to his orientation, even as it approaches the individual, is that it so clearly addresses the multiple dimensions of what it means to be human, and opens us to a contemplation of the heights to which we can aspire in our relation to all reality. The human person, in Bonaventure's view, is not a one-dimensional creature.

But if the human person is not one-dimensional, neither is the world in which that person is situated. This is a spiritual vision that opens us also to the complexity of the outside world in a culture that inclines us to think in more positivistic and one-dimensional terms. At one level, creation can be described in purely chemical terms. Even the phenomenon of human consciousness and knowledge can be described in terms of the complex chemical interactions involved, particularly in the complexity of the human brain. This is, in a sense, looking from the outside.

But, in view of this spirituality, reality has an inside also. When viewed in that way, the chemical dimension can be seen as the necessary condition for the experiences which we name, from the inside, with words such as beauty, love, and altruism. We are, indeed, bodily beings. But bodiliness in our case has developed an inside. We are embodied spirit in the world of creation. Not only can we find something of God in the outside world, but even more, we can discover stronger reflections of God by reflecting on the mystery of the interior cosmos, the human soul and its functions.

To experience a beautiful work of art from the inside is quite a different experience from describing it in terms of its formal, external elements. Only one who can re-create the glory of a Bach fugue on a splendid organ in a magnificent cathedral knows that experience of beauty from the inside. It is a very different experience from that of sitting in one's room and analyzing all the formal elements of the fugue, as it were from the outside. We are dealing with a spiritual tradition that invites us to savor the richness of the many dimensions of reality in our world and in ourselves; to come to know reality from the inside in terms of its beauty and magnificence, and not only from the outside in terms of its chemistry.

We can hardly fail to be struck by the significance that the whole of the created cosmos has in this spirituality. Given the problems that confront us today, we should be willing to ask whether what we think of as spirituality serves to alienate us from the world of creation, or whether it helps us to develop a healthy and life-giving relation to the world of God's creation. What this spiritual tradition suggests is the real possibility of being very serious about the religious significance of material reality without lapsing into some form of pantheism that would simply identify the world with God. As bodily beings with senses open to the concrete world outside us, we can find something of God already at that level.

More specifically concerning the world of creation, it is significant to encounter a vision that, from the perspective of spirituality, sees the world as a network of deeply interrelated creatures in a sense that seems to echo what the best of the modern sciences suggest about the nature of our cosmos from an empirical, physical perspective. From a spiritual perspective, this is a tradition that urges us to respect and care for all creatures, even the seemingly most insignificant. It is a spiritual tradition that sees the relational character of creation to be grounded in the mystery of the primordial community of loving relationships that Christian faith knows as the mystery of the Trinity.

The sciences, from their perspective, suggest that the ease with which we can eliminate particular members of a life system can be of far-reaching consequences. Thus, from two distinct perspectives, we are urged to be aware and to be respectful. The spiritual perspective suggests strongly that we need to shape our relation to the world in terms of a fundamentally different model than that which is so pervasive in Western culture today. A model of respect and compassion as suggested by Bonaventure's spirituality should be brought to bear on the more familiar model of domination and control.

It is one thing to speak about the revelatory power of the cosmos. It is another thing to deal with the apparent ambiguity of the message that the cosmos seems to suggest. With Bonaventure, we have a spiritual tradition that integrates the mystery of Christ deeply into our understanding of the cosmos. Christ is not an afterthought on the part of God. Rather, Christ is the key to understanding the meaning and purpose of all creation. What might seem to the scientific eye to be a cold, heartless chemical process is now seen from a spiritual perspective that allows us to say that God loves and cherishes the world and everything in it. God desires that the whole of the human race and the cosmos with humanity be brought to full fruition in a way that has been anticipated in the personal destiny of Jesus, the risen Christ. From a christological perspective, this spirituality suggests that the creative power that brings forth and sustains all of creation is a power of love that is personal, forgiving, and fulfilling. And it is above all from the mystery of Christ that we discover the most appropriate way for us to relate to each other and to the rest of the cosmos. That is the way suggested by the word *compassion* (to suffer with), which Bonaventure uses to describe the quality of divine love and the way in which that love is to be reflected by human beings in the world of creation.

We see here a spiritual tradition that opens the door for a remarkably rich form of Christian humanism, drawing all the arts and sciences into the movement of the spiritual journey. Thus it represents the real possibility that the spiritual journey need not be cut off from the other great human enterprises as these are reflected in the history of the arts and sciences.

As a spiritual tradition, it encourages us to go the way of the mind and the intellect to the fullest extent, but not to allow knowledge to be the final word about reality or about ourselves. The use of the mind in a creative and critical way is important in the area of religion and spirituality. Religious consciousness tends to resist the concerns of the intellect. However, we must be willing to reflect on the potential negative impact of well-intended but blind fanaticism that too often goes under the name of religious conviction. Particularly in a post-Enlightenment world a spirituality that invites the creative use of the intellect can play an important role in redefining what it means to be a serious believer in a world that is no longer naïve.

While this tradition urges us to recognize the importance of the intellect as a gift of God, it is yet not willing to say that knowledge is the end. The end is an ecstasy of love; love of a God who might be thought of not simply as Light, but even more in the symbolism of Fire. Ultimately reality is undergirded by a mystery of burning, creative love that ignites the fire of love in the world of creation, and above all in the human heart. There is a power throughout all of creation that enables things to unite. But that power to unite becomes a matter of free and conscious choice in humanity. It is there that we recognize it, enhance it with personal qualities, and name it with the word *love*. And it is there, above all, that the created cosmos is capable of responding in deeply personal ways to the fire of divine love. The human orientation to the divine—expressed in so many ways in our endless drive for more of truth, of goodness, of beauty, more of everything in our lives—will never come to rest except in God, and it is destined to be brought to fruition in an ecstatic union of love with God.

Selected Bibliography

Latin Texts

Doctoris Seraphici S. Bonaventurae opera omnia. 10 volumes.
  Quaracchi: Collegium S. Bonaventurae, 1882–1902.
Hugh of St. Victor. *De arrha animae.* In *Patrologia Latina,* vol. 176.
  Edited by J. P. Migne.

Studies

Bettoni, Efrem, O.F.M. *St. Bonaventure.* Translated by Angelus
  Gambatese, O.F.M. South Bend, Ind.: University of Notre
  Dame Press, 1964.
Cousins, Ewert. *Bonaventure: The Soul's Journey into God, The Tree
  of Life, The Life of St. Francis.* New York: Paulist Press, 1978.
Doyle, Eric, O.F.M. *The Disciple and the Master: St. Bonaventure's
  Sermons on St. Francis of Assisi.* Quincy, Ill.: Franciscan Press,
  Quincy University, 1983.
Gilson, Etienne. *The Philosophy of St. Bonaventure.* Translated by
  Dom I. Trethowan and F. Sheed. Paterson, N.J.: St. Anthony
  Guild Press, 1963. Now available from Franciscan Press,
  Quincy University, Quincy, Illinois.
Hayes, Zachary, O.F.M. *The Hidden Center: Spirituality and
  Speculative Christology in St. Bonaventure.* St. Bonaventure,
  N.Y.: Franciscan Institute, 1992.
Majchrzak, Colman, O.F.M. *A Brief History of Bonaventurianism.*
  Pulaski, Wis.: Franciscan Publishers, 1957.
McGinn, Bernard. *The Presence of God: A History of Western
  Christian Mysticism.* Vol. 3, *The Flowering of Mysticism: Men*

and Women in the New Mysticism, 1200–1350. New York: Crossroad, 1998.

Ratzinger, Joseph Cardinal. *The Theology of History in St. Bonaventure.* Translated by Zachary Hayes, O.F.M. Chicago: Franciscan Herald Press, 1971. Now available from Franciscan Press, Quincy University, Quincy, Illinois.

Schmucki, Octavian, O.F.M.Cap. *The Stigmata of St. Francis of Assisi: A Critical Investigation in the Light of Thirteenth-Century Sources.* Translated by Canisius Connors, O.F.M. St. Bonaventure, N.Y.: Franciscan Institute, 1991.

Texts in Translation

Habig, M., O.F.M. *Omnibus of Sources.* Chicago: Franciscan Herald Press, 1973. Now available from Franciscan Press, Quincy University, Quincy, Illinois.

English Translations of Writings of Bonaventure

Works of St. Bonaventure. 6 volumes. St. Bonaventure, N.Y.: Franciscan Institute, 1956–. Includes *On the Reduction of the Arts, Itinerarium mentis in Deum, Disputed Questions on the Mystery of the Trinity, Disputed Questions on the Knowledge of Christ, Writings Concerning the Franciscan Order, Collations on the Ten Commandments.* Each volume includes a helpful introduction to the text.

The Works of Bonaventure. 5 volumes. Paterson, N.J.: St. Anthony Guild Press, 1960–66. Includes two volumes of mystical writings, the *Breviloquium,* the *Defense of the Mendicants, Collations on the Six Days of Creation.* Now available from Franciscan Press, Quincy University, Quincy, Illinois.

Bringing Forth Christ: Five Feasts of the Child Jesus. Translated by Eric Doyle, O.F.M. Oxford: SLG Press, 1984.

What Manner of Man? Sermons on Christ by St. Bonaventure. Translated with commentary by Zachary Hayes, O.F.M. Chicago: Franciscan Herald Press, 1974. Now available from Franciscan Press, Quincy University, Quincy, Illinois.